The Love Commission

Savannah Sprites – Book One

By

Vicki Ballante

The Love Commission
Copyright 2014 by Vicki Ballante
ISBN: 978-1-61333-780-6
Cover art by Tibbs Designs

Published by Decadent Publishing Company
www.decadentpublishing.com

Printed in the United States of America

~Dedication~

To Zee Monodee who believed in me before I believed in myself.

Prologue

*E*verything changed the day Teera, Gelsey's "mother", brought her an urgent message. She stepped away from channeling rainwater into a valley devoid of life and opened up the leaf scroll, her mouth forming an 'o' in surprise. Teera waited and watched, her face serious. It read:

> *You have been summoned to the African Savannah Queen. Please travel to her palace near Choma, Zimbabwe, immediately.*
> *Sincerely,*
> *The Queen's Secretary Fairy.*

Gelsey's hands shook as she held the scroll in the sunlight. Two other fairies gathered around to peer over her wings.

To be summoned by the monarch was a huge privilege for any fairy—whether savannah, water, or sky.

"What have I done to deserve it?" she said to her friends. "Sure, I've maintained the eco-system balance in South Africa for years. I think I'm accurate and thorough. Well, I aim to be." She peered at Teera who smiled warmly at her. "But I haven't helped the animals close to extinction yet." Why would the queen want a junior fairy?

She'd often wanted to help struggling species, but without the given orders, possessed no ability or freedom to do so. Sprites often didn't interfere with extinctions. Their ultimate goal remained to preserve the earth, and their abilities matched the job.

"I have to leave." She shook her wings as if the movement could prepare her for the journey and meeting the queen.

"You'll need Smyren to accompany you. He's strong and will make sure you get there safe," Teera said. "I've brought him along. He's behind the tree."

Smyren appeared, staring at Gelsey as if she were another task to complete.

"Well, let's go. We have no time to lose." She tapped Teera and her friend's wings. She'd find shoots and leaves to eat on the way. The warmer weather would make the journey bearable.

Gelsey travelled a long distance, and her wings ached. She'd never flown so far before in such a short time. Soaring over Zimbabwe, she looked down upon a beautiful and yet barren land, neglected by human farmers and cultivators. She loved the wildness, though. Flying past the bare grasslands and perching to rest on a majestic baobab tree, she let her wings rest a little and stretched the tired tendons.

"What an adventure," she spoke to the air and Smyren who perched on a nearby bush but remained unresponsive. She screwed up a face at him—sometimes the male fairies acted so pompous.

"Time to go," he said without a smile.

She nodded and whipped up her wings into a frenzy to complete the last leg of her journey. Within a couple of hours, she neared the entrance to the queen's home constructed of an elaborate labyrinth of towering ant heaps. In some ways, the queen fairy was like the queen ant. The ants had built this home for her to have her children. The very place where Gelsey and her siblings and friends had been born.

The entrance to the palace couldn't be mistaken, and Gelsey tiptoed in, holding her breath. Inside the dull brown anthills made of packed earth, she found a high-ceilinged entrance hall and corridors and rooms, plated with gold and jewels, wall hangings woven from butterfly and dragonfly wings, and ladybird shell floor tiles. Myriad fairy servants chosen to serve the queen flitted around from room to room, wings a flutter. Her servants were taller and imposing, their noses sharper and eyes clearer than the simple earth, sea, and sky sprites she'd known.

"Are you Gelsey, the African Savannah Earth fairy?" A sweet-voiced lady servant came up and touched her wing gently with hers.

Gelsey nodded, some of the tightness in her chest disappearing as she looked into the woman's kind eyes. "Come with me. The queen has prepared a banquet for you."

Gelsey's wings fluttered at a crazy rate. *What? A banquet?* She was a young savannah fairy, who hadn't worked long on the earth and spent many a day playing around with cats and birds and all the insects distracting her from her tasks. Why her? But fairies never questioned their queen. She had the wisdom of the ages behind her because she lived forever, or at least for a very long time. None of the fairies currently living knew of her birth or of another queen before her. All of her years on the earth meant she knew more about the balance of nature than anyone else. If Gelsey had been chosen, there was good reason.

Walking into the banquet hall, her wings whirred. The servant pressed her fingers on them to ease the noise. Gelsey didn't want to draw attention to herself yet, so she took a breath to calm her nerves. But the buzz of fairies talking and eating seemed to drown out the frantic hum of her wings. No one appeared to notice her. The lady led her to the head table where the queen was seated. Still no one watched her, much to her relief. Had the queen known she couldn't handle the attention of these important fairies?

What was she to say to the queen who had birthed her but with whom she'd never spoken before?

The monarch smiled, her wings lifting a little. Close up, her face shone like damsel fly wings, her nose perfectly formed, her mouth red and full like a rose bud. She was magnificent, but Gelsey felt her presence belayed her royalty more than her appearance. She seemed to seep the wisdom of the ages out of her pores; her eyes were dark with compassion and authority.

"Take a seat, Gelsey dear."

Gelsey smiled at her warmth. The queen knew how to calm a young, nervous sprite.

The buzz continued in the room as fairies ate, everyone jovial and hopeful.

"I have a commission for you." Her face became serious, almost mournful. "This is a vital commission. I do not wish to frighten the other fairies, so I organized a banquet to drown out my words to you. Just a handful know the import of your assignment. Listen close, young fairy. The future of the earth depends on your obedience."

"It does?" The words tumbled out. How could the queen put everything on her young, frivolous shoulders?

"You have proven your worth by helping the eco-system balance in South Africa. You prevented some serious problems."

"But all I did...." She'd looked after the birds and cats and a few insects, nothing special. Her love for the creatures of the earth had been her only motive. Somehow, she knew what needed to be rescued and what had to die. Allowing creatures to perish had always been her hardest job, yet she'd known it was for the good of all in the long run.

The queen shook her head, her wings coming to rest on her side. With a deep whisper, she spoke to Gelsey. "The humans are dying out."

"Oh." Her words meant nothing to Gelsey. She didn't like many humans. They left litter she had to pick up constantly and they polluted the soil and rivers, making the fairies' lives much harder. Some humans helped nature, but they were rare. If the humans died off, it would preserve the earth.

A small smile broke the solemnity of the queen's face. "I know. Most earth, sea, and sky fairies don't care much for humans. But, they are vital to the life of the earth."

"They're not dying off. They're taking over. Their cities are growing. I don't understand."

"The good ones are dying off, and the bad ones are getting stronger."

She frowned, unsure what the queen meant.

"The humans have discovered they can still be happy without having children. If this continues, they will no longer reproduce and the good ones will die out."

So, what's the problem, and what can I do? Reserve prevented her from voicing her questioning thoughts.

"Don't withdraw. This is vital." The queen touched her hand. "Take some food while you think about what I have said."

For the first time, she noticed the feast placed before her. Flowers, roots, and leaves, cooked with gorgeous fragrances and spices made her realize the journey had built up her hunger. She tucked in, trying to fathom what the queen meant. If humans died out, the world would change in a big way. Yet, she couldn't see them becoming extinct in the near future. The queen knew best, though. She must obey. Sprites considered it a privilege to get a commission from the queen. Not many did. They usually received monthly orders from their mother. Gelsey ate with vigor, all strength and courage returning to her. When she'd washed down her meal with pure spring water, the queen touched her wing to catch her attention. Some fairies danced in the center of the room, the banquet reaching fever pitch. The queen must have chosen the noisiest moment to give her the commission.

"You are to enter the human world...as a human."

Gelsey blinked, her wings trembling against her back. Four fairies had entered the human world and only one had come back safe, having succeeded in her commission. Two others had remained human, and the last one had been killed.

"I don't understand...."

"You are a young fairy who has an amazing ability to calm down the most frightened bird or insect. I believe you will be as suitable for this commission as you are beautiful and humble.

You know you aren't perfect. Someone humble enough to admit her weaknesses would be just right for the human world. You won't lose your personality at all when you take your new form. You won't even lose your wings. They will merely remain dormant. You *will* be divested of some of your powers, though. But your power to calm down the distressed will remain. That power will enable you to succeed in your commission."

"What am I to do?"

"You are to marry a man for a year. You will find out why the humans want love and sex but not children. As you may have learned in your studies at nature school, Homo sapiens reproduce differently to fairies. They reproduce by sex between a male and female. But the species have devised several means to prevent babies from being formed in the female body even though they continue to have sex. This has lowered the reproduction rate of the creatures who are important for the balance of the earth, specifically in South Africa. For this purpose, I want you to enter into their world and feel what they feel. You are to know what it is to love a male human with their type of love. You will go at the first break of spring and will be able to return home at the start of the following spring. We will give you your own vial of fairy dust. The gold dust should be used only twice. The first time is when you find a suitable man to marry. When you find someone who is single and who cares about the balance of nature, you must sprinkle the fairy dust on his head. The magic will make him want to marry you. Once the magic has worked, you cannot find another man. He is the one for you. If you mistakenly choose a married man, you will get one more chance."

Gelsey's wings beat against her back until they ached. Become a human and marry one? How would she know what to do? And a whole year? She would miss out on spring. It had been a long, cold winter, and she wouldn't get to see or hear all the new baby birds or play with the flying ants when the rains came.

"The second time you should use the fairy dust is to come

home. You are to sprinkle the dust on the man you have chosen to make him turn away from you. He will forget every instant shared with you. He will forget his marriage, and so will everyone he knows. Then you can come home without arousing any suspicion. Ziana will explain where you are to go and what job you will take on in the human world to make you fit in there. You have a month to find this man you are to wed. While you are married to him, you need to find out from him or anyone else you meet, like other females, the reason for the humans not wanting as many children. You are to research your own emotions and those of the male's, and work out what is happening to humans to change their future."

"What if I don't find anything of importance?"

"By becoming one of them, you will automatically understand how they think and what is happening in their hearts. Although you may not comprehend in the beginning, marrying a male human will help you to understand. Well, that's what we believe."

Gelsey wasn't so sure. The queen had much more wisdom than the general fairy, but what if she didn't know everything? Fairies knew little of the human world. They had never understood humans and their strange behaviors.

"If you succeed at your commission, you will be promoted to Head Endangered Animal earth fairy for South Africa."

Gelsey gasped. To be able to save an animal from extinction had been her dream for years. But could she fulfill this commission?

"You are not obligated to take up this assignment. However, the royal palace will be very disappointed if you don't take it. You are our first choice."

She stared at the fairies dancing and talking around her. They seemed oblivious to her conversation with the queen, but she somehow knew they suspected something. Everyone relied on her. Her future depended on her obedience. If she didn't take the commission, she might never know what it was like to save a whole species herself. She might never get another chance to obtain the honor.

She nodded and took in a deep breath, her wings coming to rest on her back. "I shall take the commission."

The queen stood, a glass of dew in her hand. "Gelsey has accepted," she boomed above the din of the room, lifting the drink in a toast.

Everyone stilled, and then applause erupted. Gelsey felt as if her freckles were pricking her face. All the important palace fairies stared and cheered at her. She reveled in the attention, but in the back of her mind, an ever-increasing dread bloomed. What would it be like to be a human? What if she never came back like the other two fairies? What if she never understood why the humans chose to have fewer babies? What would this human male be like? Would she miss her home? Would she survive one whole spring and summer away from the earth and all its wonders? She had no choice. This was for the good of the earth and the animals she would save.

Chapter One

"Next spring," Gelsey whispered to herself, echoing the words stuck in her mind for the last three weeks and two days. The very ones she'd spoken in shock to the African Savannah Queen Fairy at her commission to become a human for a whole year.

"Are you talking to yourself again?" Her new boss, Marissa, bumped her elbow as she reached for a few stalks of bristle-leaved red top grasses for some height in her flower arrangement. Marissa didn't honor Gelsey's need for space. Or maybe humans had a different space bubble than fairies. She'd faced too many adaptations upon entering the human world. No wonder she was so irritable all the time.

Sighing, she worked on the arrangement while she gazed out the tiny florist's shop. People walked past their window, oblivious to her own thoughts and world.

"You're a grump today." Marissa rolled her eyes.

"I know. I'm stressing with all the funerals."

"It's part of the business of flower arranging. We do more funeral arrangements than anything else."

Gelsey wanted to say if the humans were more in touch with nature, they wouldn't die so young but bit her lip. Every day she had to stop herself from saying something to give away her roots—her whole life story. She was an earth fairy. That's where she belonged, with the fragrant soil, scented flowers, and in the sunshine and under the fresh showers. Oh, she missed the spring rains falling on her wings. Bitty, her fairy friend, would always moan at her when she shook her wings at the other fairies upon entering the tree stump homes. The spray would go over all the furniture, and there would be a collective groan from those indoors.

"Earth to Gelsey." Marissa pinched her.

"I'm sorry. I need fresh air soon."

"You always need fresh air. The air con in this shop is working fine."

"I hate air con. So stale. So fake."

"Stop complaining. At least it's cool."

If you had wings, you could cool yourself down whenever you needed. "I know. I'm sorry." She winked at Marissa.

The woman could be bossy, but she was her only friend in the human world. It seemed to take time to make friends as everyone kept so busy. From her observations in the three weeks she'd been here, the people around her usually made friends with those they worked with because work kept the focus.

Spring in the fairy world got hectic, too. She missed the activity. All because she had to do research into the humans to save the eco-system. Her old self had thrived on eco-system balance. Definitely her forte. But she'd never dealt with humans. Now she was one.

She slipped her hand into her denim skirt pocket and clamped it around the cool vial she'd hidden there. It felt good in her palm—a little bumpy with a molded metal feel.

A man walked into the florist shop. She glanced at him to gauge his age. He appeared to be early thirties like her, with an open face, small nose, and large eyes. For a human, he was pleasant to look at. He presented another opportunity to fulfill her commission because her chances were running out. If she completed the assignment, she would get her dream job in African Savannah Fairyland—the coveted job of all the earth fairies. Five days—all the time remaining to find a man to marry.

"Hi." He neared the counter, ignored Marissa, and moved

right up to her.

For once, the lack of personal space in the human world didn't suffocate her. She had no desire to pull away from him. He seemed to give off a sweet aura like a rose or a daisy.

"I need a flower arrangement for my girlfriend."

Gelsey's heart sank. So, he wasn't single. Another guy unfit to use for her commission. And this one looked good. As he grinned at her with dimples pressing his cheeks into rings and his deep-sea-blue eyes sparkling, a strange sensation—like her wings were inside her body—fluttered in her tummy.

"Well, she isn't my girlfriend yet. I was hoping to change the situation with some flowers."

Marissa sniggered and turned away to take her arrangement for the funeral to the back room.

"Well, what does she like?" Gelsey asked. "I can make up something to take her breath away."

He gave a warm smile, causing another strange flutter in her belly. "I believe you can. You look earthy, like you belong in a garden."

The tips of her fingers tingled as if she'd touched snow or frost, but instead of cold, it was a warm, pleasant sensation. The same tingle ran up her arms, and the sun seemed to beat upon her neck and cheeks. What was wrong with her? Humans had strange sensations, but this was the oddest yet.

He gave her a knowing look as if he could read her feelings. She wished she could hide behind the arrangement she worked on.

"I don't know too much about her. All I know is she likes to ride horses."

Ah, a horse human. She knew those. Many times she'd helped them because they were very in tune with nature—one of her favorite types of humans—those and the wild ones like rangers and explorers.

"She sounds good."

"Thanks. I met her when I.... You see, I install solar-powered geysers to help the environment here in Northern Kwazulu

Natal."

An environmentalist—a rare breed in South Africa where Gelsey had spent most of her fairy existence. If he installed solar-powered geysers, he kept in touch with nature, and, therefore, on the fairies' side. The man didn't have a girlfriend. Her hand went to the vial in her pocket. Five days remained to find the man she would be married to for a year, and this guy was the best single one so far. Okay, he liked another girl, but he wasn't dating her yet. And he met requirement number two for her commission—he cared about nature.

"Come back behind the counter here. I want you to help me choose the flowers for her setting." By this point, if she'd still been a fairy, her wings would be whirring with the excitement and anxiety of trying to sprinkle magic dust on him without his knowledge. Instead, her heart beat like crazy, making blood swoosh in her ears.

What if she couldn't get the fairy dust from the vial onto his head? Suppose he saw her and stopped her?

He frowned at her request but came around the counter, his dark blue gaze upon her, his eyes warm despite being blue, his expression sweet despite him being a stranger.

Controlling the inner tremble his gaze invoked, she pointed at all the containers scattered on the floor and against the wall—various flowers and greenery propped up in water-filled buckets, dry grasses sitting in metal cans. There was a huge array to choose from but nothing like the earth, where she would be surprised as she flew around a hill to find a whole new spread of color. She missed the wildness of the outdoors. The shop looked too ordered. Yet, she rejoiced that the queen had chosen her to be a florist in the human world. At least she had some reminders of what she loved from home.

"Wow, I wouldn't know where to begin."

She smiled at his lost expression, taking in the full effect of him close up. The male could compare to a beautiful autumn sunrise. She'd never been so enamored with the species before.

"Take a careful look at each one. Smell them, touch them,

and listen to them. Use all your senses to work out whether they belong to your girl or not."

He glanced at her, eyebrows raised, then bent down toward the pink gerberas—hot pink flowers with many narrow, busy petals. The girl he liked must have a joyful, giving personality. She felt bad for taking him away from the woman, but he would only be gone for a year. Human love did seem a little strange, though. They made such a hoopla about it. In the three weeks she'd been a human, she'd heard enough on TV and from people around her to learn how much their lives revolved around the emotion.

As he rose with a flower in his hand, she moved behind him and took out the vial, popped the lid with a loud suction sound, stood on her tiptoes, and sprinkled it over his head just as he spun around to face her.

"I'm sorry," she whispered. "It's for the best."

"What was that?" He stared at the fine mist of sparkling gold in the air and then watched some settle on the blossom in his hand. "Wow, it looks beautiful. What flower is this?"

"It's a pink gerbera." She tried to keep the swirl of excitement, fear, and tension from her face. She nodded and took the flower from him.

"I can make up an arrangement with more of the pink, also some yellow goldenrod and leafy-green ruscus. They look gorgeous together with strong color contrasts."

"And this gold sprinkle, too?"

She nodded, wondering how long it would take for the dust to work in making him want her. What would it be like? Could she do this? The thoughts took her breath away. How would it feel to be admired by a man? What was love like? Would she be able to love him back? Did humans always have such strong and confusing emotions?

"Give me ten minutes, and your arrangement will be ready. You're welcome to look around in the meantime. Maybe you can find another gift for her like a teddy bear or trinket."

She turned away from him, wishing somehow she could

move back the clock and be a young, innocent fairy again and not this grown-up one who had to obey difficult orders. Oh, to be carefree, to fly from tree to tree, flower to flower; to pick up the little, speckled eggs on the ground, which had fallen from the nests and put them back without the mother birds noticing. Then to see the mother bird—

"Excuse me." He touched the small of her back. A warm shiver pulsed through her at his simple touch. "What's your name again?"

"I didn't tell you my name. It's Gelsey."

"Are you magic? I don't believe in magic but there's something...."

"Every woman has a certain magic." She fluttered her eyelashes at him.

"I have to go."

"What about your arrangement?" She coughed as her throat constricted. He was leaving? What if the fairy dust hadn't worked and she failed her commission? She would never get to save the wild cats from extinction. Only one fairy had entered the human world before and succeeded. If she failed, she would forever be a disappointment in her own eyes—and the rest of fairyland.

"I can't." His face froze in horror. He turned and ran out of the shop and down the arcade.

Marissa came through. "What on earth happened to the customer?"

"I don't know. He looked spooked."

Marissa gasped. "What's this on the floor?"

"No, don't—" Marissa swiped some fairy dust off the counter with her forefinger. She brought it to her nose and sniffed. Gelsey held her hand over her mouth to suppress a guffaw. If a woman touched the fairy dust, something marvelous would happen to her. Teera, her "mother" fairy, had told her of such things. She should avoid anyone touching the dust in case of discovery, but it caused no harm unless she sprinkled it on the wrong single man. Maybe she'd done just that. Maybe he wasn't single after all, or maybe he wasn't in tune with nature.

"I need to sweep it up." With trembling hands, she picked up a dustpan and brush and collected the fairy dust in case she needed to find another man. Marissa helped her.

"Where did you find this stuff? It makes the flowers come alive." The rather dumpy woman with boring, short, charcoal hair transformed into a beauty—her face took on a glow.

Ah, fairy dust. For the first time in her life, Gelsey had been given her own vial. She understood what made all the fairies covet the substance. Oh, the power of it.

"This is my own glitter," she said, remembering she had to keep her cover. "It's for my crafting. It's very expensive, so I can't lose any of it."

"Of course. Wish I could have some in the shop though. Where do you get it?"

Before Gelsey could come up with an answer, the phone rang, saving her from pure disaster. Fairies didn't lie to one another. But, oh she forgot...she was human. She could lie without batting an eyelid. She just had. And wasn't her whole persona at this point a lie?

Chapter Two

*E*van struggled to get the image of the beautiful flower woman, Gelsey, out of his mind. He'd jumped in the car to go back to his office on Patterson Street to fetch some more supplies for an installation which he didn't need right away, just to have something else to think about besides her. His friend Sandy, who loved horses, was special, but something drew him to this florist. Sure, his first glimpse of her had taken his breath away. Stunning with her—what color hair was it?— chestnut-brown tresses. Her green, green eyes resembled the new leaves of spring. Her skin was creamy and sprinkled with cinnamon freckles and flushed healthy with rosy cheeks. And the way she spoke—as if she came from another world, a happy, carefree, poetic world, not the stark, survival-of-the-fittest world he'd grown up in.

He'd worked hard for ten years to get what? Just another sales position. Sure, he believed in what he sold, knew the importance of saving electricity and using the earth's natural resources, but times were tough. No one had the money to buy solar panels and solar-powered geysers. People scraped by and, although his products would save money for them in the end, very few were willing to pay the price when times were their leanest in years.

School had been a nightmare, and he'd dropped out of

university due to his intense aversion to study and a rocky few years of dating. Young and careless, he'd thought he could earn a science degree without studying. He'd wasted years with shallow women, all for nothing.

Just when he'd found someone worth settling down with, a sweet thing at a florist he knew nothing about, distracted him. Could her sense of mystery be what intrigued him so much? He had to find out.

A strange sensation washed over him, like a tingling starting from the top of his head and over his face and then shoulders, to end at the tips of his fingers and toes.

A clear vision of her face flashed before him so he could barely concentrate on driving. He pulled up on the side of the road outside an office block.

How come it had taken so long to find her? Meeting her was his destiny. The purpose of his life set in his mind—to love this woman and care for her.

She must be new in Newcastle, South Africa. Although he didn't know everyone in the small industrial city in the northern-most part of the province of Kwazulu Natal, he would have noticed her for sure. She would stand out from any crowd, her beauty so compelling.

There was no way he could ever live without her another day of his life. She must be his. His desire to possess her wasn't intense as much as all-inclusive. His mind, his feelings, and his body knew she was the woman for him. He'd never been so sure of anything in his life before. Good thing he hadn't bought flowers for Sandy.

The arrangement!

He'd rushed out of the shop because a need to kiss the florist had overwhelmed him so much, he'd been afraid of his own feelings. He'd always been a rather reserved man, part of the reason his dating adventures had proven quite rocky. It took four or five dates before he ventured to even kiss a woman. Many hadn't waited so long. Never had he wanted to kiss a woman he'd just met. Had she bewitched him? For a man who thrived on the scientific method as a basis for most of his theories about life, the idea a woman could put a spell on him didn't sit well.

He'd dashed out of the shop to escape the weird, out-of-control sensation, but distance hadn't provided the answer.

What should he do? Go back to her?

Of course.

Throwing his usual cautious, logical nature to the wind, he turned the car around in three quick maneuvers and drove back to the florist.

He rode down Murchison Street and backed up toward the arcade off Scott Street. Strangely enough, although it was month's end when the town teemed with traffic and people, he spotted three empty parking places. He drove straight into one, stopped his car, and resisted the urge to sprint toward the little store tucked away in an arcade. He braced himself, sucked in a breath, and walked inside, sure he gave the appearance of logic, good common sense, and easy confidence. The chestnut-haired belle looked up from a computer screen, and her face lit up at the sight of him, giving him a confidence boost.

"Hi," he said. He hadn't dreamed her up after all. A part of him had wondered if the difficult last few months had finally gotten to him. He hadn't sold enough solar heaters to pay for his bond payment the last two months unless he cut into some savings, which wasn't an option.

She smiled, and her gentle gaze eased the tension that had wound up his body for some time. This woman wielded a power over him.

"Are you taking the arrangement?" Her voice rang out in the shop like music.

This was the first time he'd registered the clear bell of her voice—like the most glorious music or the sound of the birds in the break of dawn during spring. His house had a lavish, almost wild garden that attracted many bird species. The cacophony of their song in the morning always soothed his spirit. The beauty before him spoke like their songs. Her rich, copper-toned locks glowed like a sunset behind a cloud.

"Where do you live?" he asked.

"Why do you ask?" A pink tinge made her cheeks pretty and desirable to touch.

"Write your address on the card and have the flowers sent there."

"Oh...thank you. I love flowers. I miss them." The wistful, almost pained expression on her face made him want to send her ten arrangements.

"You do? Is that possible?" He couldn't understand why she'd miss them. She worked with them every day.

"I miss having my own."

He laughed. "There are lots of things I would like to get you."

"Why?"

"You're beautiful—the most stunning woman I've ever seen."

A healthy blush spread over her cheeks, adding to their rosy complexion. "What about your woman friend who cares for horses?"

He came up to her, taking her hand, which felt as soft as silk. "I know we've just met, and you don't know me, but would you be willing to come out to supper with me tonight?

She nodded, the large pupils darkening her green eyes to pools in a forest. Her gaze transported him into a leafy glen in some faraway location away from the hustle and bustle of life, fresh and lively. When had he become so poetic?

"You have a strange effect on me."

She pressed her lips together and sighed. "I can see."

He pulled away, his hand aching from losing contact with her. "I'm sorry."

She shrugged. "It's fine."

He didn't want it to be fine. He wanted her to feel the passion, too. Very unlikely she also would experience what he had in such a short moment, but he would woo her. Phew, this determination was foreign to a man who'd been rather purposeless and *laissez faire* most of his life. Never had he wanted or needed something so badly, and been so sure about it.

"I'll do whatever you wish," she said, shifting her focus toward a bunch of flowers on the counter. She fingered a petal with reverence as though it were a child's earlobe.

Her gaze alighted on him again, filled with sadness. He could ask what had caused it, but refrained from prying into her private thoughts. He hadn't reached the point where he could meet all her needs. Was it possible? He'd never been able to meet the needs of any of the women he'd dated. They'd all been too complex.

Yet a desire birthed in him to be there for her, to ravish her in every way, to meet every need she possessed. He wanted to fathom the dark recesses of her being and touch them with a part of his soul. Their oneness would meet her needs, would satisfy her and complete him.

He instinctively picked up her hand and kissed the soft, fleshy inner valley of her palm. Sweetness tingled upon his lips and shot into him, almost jolting like an electric shock but without the pain. After-burn remained, simmered inside him.

"See you tonight. Outside your home? May I take the address?"

She nodded, her pupils large, her mouth silent.

"Gelsey, come here, please," the other florist called. "Oh, sorry. I didn't mean to disturb you...." She glanced at his hand still holding hers and promptly spun to return to the back room of the florist shop.

"Gelsey, what a beautiful name."

She laughed. "Marissa's going to lose her eyebrows."

"What did you say?" He laughed at her funny expression and warmed at the tinkling sound of her mirth. "How come?"

"I don't often have customers holding my hand."

"I've never done anything like this before." He stared into her eyes, longing to gauge her feelings for him.

"I suspected as much." She tapped his knuckles with her fingertip. "I've never had anyone treat me like this before either."

Her gaze held mischief and a little vulnerability. This girl deserved to be loved more than any other he'd known.

"See you tonight," he said with a sigh. "I'd better go." *Before I take her in my arms right this second and kiss the life out of her. Then I'll make her lose her job.*

ଔ

Being stuck inside at dusk tortured Gelsey, but she had to enhance her appearance for the date. Being a fairy, the sun, the earth, rivers, and the air had given her a natural glow, but humans remained indoors most of their lives. Their skin grew dull, and their hair lost its sheen. She stared at herself in the mirror and sighed. Tears came to her eyes, but she blinked them away. Hunger, a sensation shared by fairies and humans alike, gave its familiar tug at her stomach. He would be here in a few minutes and they would eat, but the food wouldn't take away the unease inside her.

She so wished she hadn't sprinkled the fairy dust on him. The way he looked at her, as if he needed her more than his own breath, made her want to run far away. What had the queen been thinking? Although she had been a human for three weeks, in this short time and especially today, she knew playing with a human's emotions was a dangerous thing. Their feelings had a direct effect on their health and could shorten their life.

She closed her eyes, remembering the meeting with the queen, the upheaval to her life from that day still cutting a sharp pain into her chest with every breath.

Sighing, she opened her eyes and faced the mirror. She still had the two tiny bumps on her back where her wings tucked in under her human skin, almost imperceptible to the human eye. They reminded her of what she'd left behind, of the captivity she'd entered into. She swallowed to relieve the choking ache swelling up in her throat.

Oh, how she longed to use her wings again, to fly up into the sky and peer down at the birds in flight, watching their patterns below her.

Just a year, that's all. She brushed her hair until it shone, pinched her cheeks to bring some color back, and walked to the front door. At that moment, she heard a knock. The ache in her throat grew bigger. She sucked in a deep breath and braced herself for the scary unknown.

Chapter Three

*E*van clenched his fist after knocking on Gelsey's door. Maybe this was all a crazy dream and he would wake up with the same life as before, without this woman in it. Could he handle the emptiness?

Just to prove him wrong, the door opened and there she stood, a pixie-like smile on her face, her cheeks flushed and her fiery hair resting on her shoulders, like spun silk, delicious and out of this world. Could there be anyone to match her beauty? Her eyes twinkled with some bottled-up emotion then a shadow passed over them.

He sucked in a breath. The effect she had on him rendered him speechless for a second. She even smelled good—like freshly mowed grass on a summer's day tinged with the whiff of the first spring blossoms on an apple tree. "Are you ready, Gelsey?"

She nodded, almost as if she had waited for this moment and resigned herself to it. He had to stop thinking the worst—that she didn't really want him. This was their first date anyway. *Give it time.*

He linked arms with her once she locked up and led her to his car. The Ford Bantam utility vehicle didn't look the most romantic, but at least it was fairly new and had enough space in the front for the two of them.

"I'm vegetarian," was the first thing she said.

He turned to her, suppressing a laugh at her seriousness. "Um, no problem. I'm sure the new John Dory's at the strip mall will offer some vegetarian options on the menu. You don't have to have fish or seafood. Or we could go Chinese."

She frowned at him as if confused.

"Fried rice, sweet and sour pork. Oh goodness, I'm sorry. Well, they have vegetable spring rolls with fried rice. Sweet and sour sauce is to die for."

"I'm willing to give seafood a try."

"Are you sure?"

She nodded, her chin firming up. He touched her hand briefly, hoping to calm the turmoil he sensed inside of her.

She gasped and pulled away. *What?* She'd seemed so interested in him at the shop. He'd planned so much for tonight. Maybe he'd been too hopeful or even presumptuous.

"How was your day?" he asked as they drove to Amajuba Mall where they'd set up the restaurant last month.

"Fine, thanks."

"What's troubling you?"

Once again she appeared surprised at his concern as if she hadn't experienced someone caring before.

"I...I'm just tired. My job is good, but I miss the outdoors."

"You're an outdoorsy person? I've never gone for camping and the big outdoors, but I'm willing to give it a try." He gave her a wink. All of a sudden, being outdoors with her seemed like a true adventure. He'd been so busy making a living that he hadn't lived. He let out a shaky breath. How come he'd only just realized it?

"The sun is a healing balm," she said with pure conviction.

"I'm quite pleased with the sun as it gives energy. Part of my business."

"I know." She nodded, confidence coming back in the upward tilt of her chin and the cheeky flicker of her long lashes.

"You're observant."

"Observant is my second name."

He laughed. He could bear with her moods when she became feisty in between. Since when could he handle a woman's moods or care what was buried under the layers?

"I'm going to find out all about you and make you happy."

The shadow passed over her face again, but then she smiled, a large grin that hid something. Maybe her sense of mystery is what attracted him.

The evening was going to be a roller-coaster ride, but he felt ready for the adrenalin rush. Oh, so ready.

ভ

Gelsey thought her head would spin out of control. The strange warm sensations in her tummy made her loathe to eat despite the hunger pangs. Is this what the human love emotion felt like? Something about this man—the way he spoke to her, the way he looked at her, as if she was so important, as if he cared how she felt, stirred the strange feelings. Even her fairy friends hadn't connected with a spot deep inside of her. She wished she could tell him of the turmoil in her soul, of the world she had left behind, and of how she missed her home and her friends. Maybe he would care. Maybe he would help her and let her leave early. He would tell her all about human love, so she didn't have to be trapped a whole year.

"Um, tell me about love," she said once they were seated opposite each other at the fish restaurant. She could somehow stomach eating seafood but, being an earth fairy, couldn't bear to eat the animals she'd spent so many years helping out. According to Ziana, she would be human and forget most of her life as a fairy. The thought of losing all touch with her past had prompted a deep fear in her, and she'd determined never to forget. Thankfully, somehow, she could remember almost everything.

She'd skipped lunch, and the smell of seafood cramped her already empty stomach. Evan had sent her whole day in a crazy direction. She'd been quite happy to spend the rest of her year working in the florist, making pretty arrangements, meeting people, and asking them questions. She wasn't ready for this marriage thing and had no idea what it entailed.

Evan stared at her. "Love?"

"Yes, tell me how it felt when you fell in love. It seems it happens more than once in a man's life."

His eyes twinkled. "This is my first time."

He looked right into her, his gaze giving off some magic as though he'd been the one to sprinkle fairy dust. He'd almost bewitched her. If she hadn't been a fairy, she would be falling into this love thing right this second.

"Why do you ask?"

She shrugged. "I didn't expect you to answer in such a way."

"You cut to the chase, don't you?"

"I beg your pardon?"

"You're a very innocent person. It's as if you've been sheltered from so much."

"I've lived for the earth and the environment. Love hasn't featured in my life."

He took hold of her hand and squeezed it. "I'd like to show you what it's like."

His gaze seemed to hold depths like the ocean. Depths of knowledge and something she'd never fathomed before. Right then, she wanted to experience love with this man.

"I hardly know you."

"Me, too." He traced her palm with his thumb.

Shivers ran through her as if she'd stepped into a cool pond when the spring sun warmed her after a cold winter. The cool water would take her breath away yet invigorate her, just like his simple touch on her hand.

He smiled, reassuring her with its warmth. She studied his masculine shape and longed to feel each part of his body beneath her fingertips, to explore it. As much as she loved to explore a cave or an overgrown forest with all its treasures inside.

"I want you so much," he whispered just as a waitress came to their table.

"What can I order for the love birds?" Her face held scorn.

Gelsey's neck heated. How come love was sometimes looked down upon in the human world?

"We haven't looked at the menu yet," Evan said.

She rolled her eyes. "Fine." She walked off.

Had there been a vibe from her? Gelsey blocked it out. Negativity would hamper her research. She had to go with the flow of this "love" thing.

They chose their food and ordered it then Gelsey looked at Evan with expectation.

"I brought you something." He sighed. "I know it might seem crazy to you."

Like everything about this doesn't seem crazy enough? "I'd like to hear," she prompted, taking his hand to assure him. This was it. No going back. Curiosity egged her on, making this commission seem way easier than she'd thought.

"Do you ever just know something for sure like you've never known it before?"

She shook her head. All she knew were the commission given her and the promotion waiting at the end. Nothing else mattered. "I don't understand."

"When I met you, I knew you were the one for me. It sounds crazy, and I understand if this scares you off, but something is compelling me to say this right now." He bent down and fumbled for something in his pocket. Gelsey knew he'd bought an engagement ring. She'd already studied up about the human rituals. The fairy dust had worked—Ziana said it wouldn't take longer than a day to bewitch the poor man.

How wicked had she become, manipulating a human's emotions? She'd let some birds and insects die before to keep the earth cycle in perfect balance. This was all part of it, but somehow she wondered if she'd done something really bad by the way she'd used him. She looked away at the mural on the wall of beautiful creatures under the sea, her heart calming. He'd forget her after she sprinkled the fairy dust over him the second time. Nothing wrong then. She would in no way influence his life for better or worse.

Her gaze returned to Evan. Bent forward, eyes shifting side-to-side, he gripped the ring between his trembling forefinger and thumb.

"Gelsey, will you marry me?"

Right then, the waitress came up to them and squealed out loud. "Everyone, he's proposing to her. In our restaurant." The cynical woman seemed to have taken a sudden interest in their love.

Gelsey gave a broad smile. Everything had worked out perfectly. "I will. Yes."

Evan's eyes popped open wide. "That's wonderful."

Applause broke out from the serving staff and the people seated at the tables surrounding them. Gelsey looked around, smiling at everyone, pleased at the attention. Fairies were gregarious creatures and hung around in crowds. This one-on-one had an almost suffocating feel to it. But the crowd wouldn't rescue her from the task ahead, whatever it consisted of. Could she still feel this pleasant "love" feeling for a whole year?

After everyone returned to their meals, Evan slid the ring onto her left "ring" finger, where she'd learned it belonged. The metal felt cool and hard against her skin. The central diamond blinked like the sun on a pool of water. She fiddled with the rock with its smooth and sharp edges. A fascinating substance found in palaces in her world.

"Are you sure about this?" He let go of her hand and tucked into his meal.

"Yes, I'm sure."

"I didn't expect you.... This boldness filled me...." He laughed.

"Why did you think I'd turn you away?" She enjoyed watching the expressions on his face, his eyes darkening with emotion as she spoke.

"We haven't known each other for long."

"That's what marriage is for, isn't it? To discover one another?"

"Nowadays, couples date and get to know each other first before they commit to forever."

"But marriage isn't forever."

He frowned and looked down. Clearly, she'd said something wrong. No human lived forever. Marriage had to die in the end. And many couples got divorced in the human world. Marriage wasn't an all-powerful bond unable to get broken. What a relief to her.

"One day at a time. When do you want to get married?"

"Tomorrow." The sooner Gelsey's commission began, the sooner she could go back home.

He coughed and stared at her, once again surprised by her response. What if he wanted to stall this?

"What about a ceremony, bridesmaids, flowers, and a white dress?"

"I don't need those things."

"If I wasn't so sure, I would say 'no', but because I don't want to lose you, I'll agree. I will arrange the papers tomorrow, but we might have to wait a couple of days."

She bit her lip, her wings aching against her back. She longed to spread them out again and soar with the air currents. Instead, she tucked into her seafood, enjoying the unusual flavors. The fish and crustaceans had to die to feed the humans, she understood that and seemed to accept it. The food sustained her and gave her new energy. It seemed she hadn't been taking in enough protein in her diet. From here on, she would move away from vegetarian no matter how hard it would be.

They ate their meal, talking about Evan's university experiences and all the jobs he'd tried. He acted surprised when she said she'd only ever been a florist. Trying to come up with her childhood experiences would prove difficult. It seemed these humans wanted to share many details of their lives with one another. Another time she would share a few of her fairy experiences—the ones applicable to a human. Enough thought and turmoil for one night. When Evan took her home, she gladly walked toward her door. She took out her keys, but he held her by her waist, stopping her.

"What's wrong, Evan?"

He didn't speak. Instead, his gaze focused on her mouth. Was he waiting for her to say something?

"Oh, thank you so much for the meal. I love seafood."

He smiled but his face drew closer to hers. Heat sprinkled over her at his closeness. He was about to kiss her. She'd seen a human kiss once while saving a domestic cat from being killed by a neighboring dog. The couple had stood by the front door, just like Evan and she were, and their mouths had connected for a long time, like the touch of an insect on a pond, suspended, causing little ripples. She'd walked away, almost disgusted with their strange behavior.

Somehow, everything seemed different. Something rose up within her—a hunger for his skin to touch hers. When his mouth rested on hers, tingles and warmth flooded her body. She wrapped her arms around his shoulders, pulling him closer. Their lips seemed to dance together with unplanned movements, each one a drum beat stirring up something powerful in her body and soul. Here was a magic she'd never known. Had any fairy experienced this before? Did they know what kissing felt like?

Much to her disappointment, he pulled away but placed his palm on her cheek. "I'll see you tomorrow, my love." His nose touched hers, and she tried to kiss him again, but he pulled away.

"Kissing can wait." His eyes held a tease.

He drove away, leaving her standing by her front door. For a minute she felt lost, unable to remember what to do next. Then she laughed at herself. Fumbling with the key, she went inside and lay down on her bed.

Strange dreams punctuated her sleep—visions of flying up a mountain, something she'd never done. She swam in the sea like a sea fairy and had a stomach swollen with human child. The last one made her jump up with a start. What if she did become pregnant? The queen or Ziana hadn't mentioned the possibility. All Ziana had said was she should take a special pill from the start of her time in the human world. The pill would stop her from having a baby, just as the humans were in a habit of doing. Ziana obviously knew she would never fall pregnant if she took the medicine. At least she was safe from bearing a human child. If she bore a child, she would be stuck as a human much longer, if not forever.

Ziana had also told her to study sex. She'd read some articles on the Internet and watched a few videos, but they'd horrified her so much she hadn't spent much time on them.

Kissing was fine but Evan would expect more. Sweat trickled down her temples. She rose and walked to the bathroom to wash her face.

Being a human, she shouldn't be afraid of sex. It was a natural process of human reproduction. The act just seemed so bizarre. The animal mating habits were straightforward. Maybe the cats could get a little noisy, but there weren't all these different techniques and ways to do things to make it more pleasurable. Why should it be pleasurable? It was done to make children.

Herein lay the whole question behind her commission. She'd become the guinea pig. The experiment.

Tears came to her eyes. Did the queen know how much this would hurt? How confused she would feel? Afraid and lost? No fairy would ever understand. Neither would a human. She was totally alone. Gripping her arms around her abdomen, she stared at her reflection in the bathroom mirror. Her hair stood up on one side, flat on the other. Her eyes appeared like two murky pools full of algae and filth. Even her cheeks appeared more hollow than usual. Ugh, she looked awful! Loneliness had never featured in her world. She'd been too busy and there'd always been winged friends around to talk to, to laugh and sing with.

The emotion felt like a cold, heavy blanket resting upon her, seeping its icy tendrils right down to her bones. She went back to bed but couldn't sleep for hours. Eventually, she fell into a fitful sleep.

Chapter Four

The next day at the florist shop, Gelsey didn't see Evan at all. Toward the end of the day, she couldn't keep still, pacing from one end of the shop to the other.

Marissa watched her with curiosity. "You're very agitated. What's up?"

"Nothing." How could she tell her friend if the marriage didn't happen, she had failed her commission? The thought sank into her. Failing her commission would mean no promotion, and the other sprites pitying her, thinking she was incapable, but maybe it would be better. She could forego the next year in the human world and return to her simple life of helping the small creatures and the balance of the eco-system in the grasslands and suburbs of South Africa.

"Is it about the man who almost kissed you yesterday by the counter?"

"I suppose."

Marissa grinned. "It's quite a pleasure to see you interested in someone."

"For you, yes." She made her mouth form a squiggly shape.

"He's left you on a string?"

"Not exactly. I'm just worried he's not going to go through with it."

Marissa stared at her left hand. "Is that what I think it is?"

Gelsey smiled at her, heat beating against her cheeks. "Um, yes."

"You met the guy yesterday?"

"I did."

"And he proposed to you? And you accepted?"

Gelsey nodded. Surely, Marissa would understand. She seemed pleased Gelsey had found someone.

"You must have lost your mind." She grabbed Gelsey by the outer arms and shook her, making her teeth rattle. "This guy could be a swindler, after your life policy. He'll marry you and kill you, then pocket your insurance."

Gelsey laughed. "Nonsense, he's crazy about me. He wouldn't kill me."

Marissa shook her head. "Listen to me. I know you're naïve, but really, have you got no sense? You can't marry a guy the first day you meet him."

"Why not?"

"Because marriage is a commitment. It's not easy to get out of. It hurts to break up. I should know. You don't just jump at these things. Why am I saying this? You know it. You're just not thinking straight."

Gelsey sighed. She wished she could explain her commission to Marissa and how the fairy dust had worked its magic on Evan.

"I know what I'm doing. I'm sure this is the way for me." Although she couldn't be totally sure she'd chosen the right single man, she knew she had to do this.

"I hope you're going to have a long en—"

Evan walked through the doorway, swishing hot air in from outside. Her wings wanted to flutter behind her head to cool her down. Instead, she felt a strange ache on her back. They should have gotten rid of her wings temporarily. She was supposed to be human, but fairy still remained embedded in her.

Marissa stared at Evan, obvious disapproval written all over her face.

His eyes lit up with a huge grin. Gelsey was stunned at how his appearance had changed since yesterday—his face shone, his eyes darkened with purpose, and he seemed to stand more erect and strong. Was it the fairy dust or the magic of human love?

"Everything is sorted. I spoke to my lawyer friend who got our papers ready today. It's an absolute miracle. We can get married tomorrow."

Marissa gave a loud sigh and disappeared to the back of the shop.

"She doesn't approve."

"I can imagine."

"I don't understand. If two people have love, what's to stop them from being together?"

He grasped her hand. "Exactly what I think. I've never thought that until I met you. I just have some explaining to do to my mother." He laughed. "She'll struggle to understand why a guy who lacks commitment marries a girl he hardly knows. Yet I feel like I've known you for years."

She smiled. How could he feel he'd known her? Over a month ago, she was in St. Lucia, helping a struggling bird population. Did this love make humans stupid? Pushing aside her inner conflict, she glanced at him. Once again, his gaze poured warm liquid into her, driving away the doubts.

But it would just be a short time. The fear and loneliness would encompass her when she found herself alone.

"One more night sleeping alone," he said as if he read her thoughts.

"One more." Would she survive with someone else always there? Someone who didn't know her roots and her destiny?

"Will you be able to take a few days off from work?" He leaned against the counter, fingering a dry grass arrangement. "I want to take you somewhere for our honeymoon. Three nights, that's all I ask."

"Um...it's short notice."

"Just take it," Marissa yelled from the back room. She marched in and pointed a finger at Evan. "You'd better look after her, mister whatever your name is. I've only known her for a month, but I know she's a sensitive, innocent soul. You'd better not mar her for life, and if she gets killed, I'll know it was you."

Evan laughed. "Why would I hurt her?"

"You think this is some crazy fairy tale?"

Gelsey gasped. *What?* The two points on her back tingled. Did Marissa know?

"Well, marriage is not a joke. It's real life, and after you've seen each other at your worst, you'll learn what it is to really love someone or you'll discover you don't know how." She propped her hands on her hips. "And if you don't know how, you're in big trouble and so is Gelsey. So, you'd better learn fast because it's not all butterflies in the tummy and romantic kisses. It's getting by without killing one another."

Maybe fairy tale was an expression in the human world. Humans didn't believe in fairies. Well, very few of them did, and those who did believe probably had never seen one. Sprites were masters at remaining invisible.

Evan shrugged. "My parents are still together."

"Mm-hmm. Gives me a tiny glimmer of hope."

"So love is only good in the beginning?" Gelsey pressed a finger to her lips. In the last few days, she'd collected some vital data for her commission. But none of it made any sense.

Evan tickled her palm. "Don't listen to her."

Gelsey nodded, but Marissa's words confused her. The humans seemed enamored with love, but if it let so many of them down, why did they go for it? Maybe the disappointment was the reason for not wanting children so much anymore. Could this be her first real clue for her commission?

"I'll see you early tomorrow morning."

"Where will we live?" Gelsey hadn't even considered those details.

Evan gazed at her as if in deep thought. "If you're keen, my house is big. It has a swimming pool and beautiful garden."

Gelsey squealed. "I've missed having a garden."

"Then we shall live there. I'll help you pack your belongings."

"It won't take long. I live a simple life."

Ignoring Marissa who watched the couple from the corner of

her eye while she completed an arrangement, Evan kissed Gelsey tenderly on the lips. Her toes seemed to curl upward. The softness of his mouth playing with hers made the loneliness and fear of the night before evaporate like the mist at midday. But, according to Marissa, the feeling wouldn't last. Yes, human love seemed like spring or a beautiful sunrise—way too short.

ᛒ

Evan took a walk to the bank from the florist to sort out some shuffling of funds.

He hated to leave Gelsey, but she was at work and he'd already booked her away with very short notice. His impulsiveness seemed to disturb Marissa. If he wasn't so at peace within himself, he would be, too.

Flitters of fear and doubt passed over Gelsey's face at times. She didn't trust him totally. Her trust would come with time, he assured himself.

He wanted to give her new sensations she'd never experienced before. Images of her in his bed, naked and beautiful, swirled around in his head. He had already planned so many ways of doing foreplay with her—of getting her to her peak. The woman stirred longings in him he'd ignored for years. About time he let loose and enjoyed a woman's body.

He'd have to wait one more night. Tonight, he could take her to his home and give her a feel for their future together, but no, he wanted it to be at a special place, away from their mundane lives. He wanted to woo her with such a huge bang she'd be unable to resist him every single day.

He would win her heart completely, even if it took him years, because deep inside, he knew she hadn't given him her heart. He couldn't fathom why she would marry him. Curiosity? Loneliness? Maybe she'd never been asked before and was afraid she would remain single forever. He suspected she didn't possess a sinister motive. Her innocent eyes gave away her purity but no love. Although she spoke of love, he didn't think she'd known it before.

Entering the bank, he waited on the comfy chair for a consultant.

Evan could kick his ridiculous, miserly self. He'd struggled with his bond for so long but never considered using up his retrenchment benefit from his previous job to sort out his debt. Maybe he'd been hoping for a windfall to come, but now that Gelsey was going to live in his home, he wanted to make sure it would remain a stable environment for her. His late payments for the bond could be sorted out, and he could put in a bit extra to tide him over for a few months.

Tonight, he would sell some stocks and put a few of his man toys for sale on the online shop, Bid or Buy. Selling some clutter would cover the honeymoon to the Drakensberg Mountains Cathedral Peak. Gelsey had probably gone there many times before—most Natalians knew the place and had either stayed at the resort or entered the reserve for a day hike or visit. The tourist attraction hotel and several other resorts were nestled in a valley surrounded by layers of majestic mountains hugging the valley in a semi-circle of magnificence. Walks in the area would offer sights of unusual rock formations and waterfalls as well as birdlife and even bushman paintings nearby.

He craved time out in nature—he always had but allowed the burdens of life to stop him from spending money on those luxuries. Maybe he'd been so busy saving for a rainy day he'd forgotten to enjoy the sunshine of the present.

Joy made him want to do a happy dance right in the bank with the harried customers watching. Having a woman to care about had loosened something wound tight within him. He felt as free as a kid again.

Chapter Five

*M*arissa had closed shop early to take Gelsey to buy a wedding dress, muttering the whole way about the craziness of it all.

As Gelsey stood in front of her mirror to see how she looked in the milk-white dress, twenty minutes before Evan would pick her up for their small court ceremony, she stared at herself, wondering what all the fuss was about. Maybe humans enjoyed beautifying themselves like the flowers did in spring, dressed up for the bees and insects to pollinate them.

Did she look elaborate enough? Without wings, she wasn't her true self. Yet somehow, the vulnerable, haunted expression gazing back at her gave her a certain beauty. Her hair shone today, curling onto her shoulders and down her back to her waist. She had no makeup or jewelry. The dress carried some glittery beads and lace on the bodice and high waistband. Gathered chiffon straps lay on her shoulders, tapering in at the dipped neckline. She wore strappy high-heeled sandals, though they made walking a challenge. But she would learn. She'd navigated mountains and caves and climbed difficult trees and creepers.

Forget your old life. Ziana had stressed she shelve her fairy memories for a whole year and jump with two feet into her new world. Taking a deep breath, she punched in Evan's number on her phone.

"I'm ready," she said, surprised how much fear shook her voice.

"I'm on my way. Have you packed a bag for three nights?"

"Yes."

The doorbell rang minutes later. She smiled despite the butterflies and moths flapping in her stomach.

She opened the door. "Have you been waiting for me?"

"I was in my car. I battled to get to sleep last night."

"Thankfully, the exhaustion knocked me out. The previous night wasn't so good."

"I can see you slept well. Your face is glowing." He came to her, his hands clasping her waist. He kissed her, running his hands down the dip and over the width of her hips. Goose bumps ran up her spine. As if on cue, his fingers tickled her back in time to the fluttering of her heart. His kiss deepened, and she dove into a deep pool of warm liquid pleasure. Breath seemed to evade her, as if he were the only air she needed.

She pulled back, gasping. "I haven't even seen what you look like."

He opened his arm to pose.

"You look good." Black and white contrasted crisply against his dark brown hair and pale skin. So that was a penguin suit. It sure resembled one of those aquatic birds. Yet, he held a dignity no waddling penguin could know. His back stood erect, his eyes strong and determined in their almost-black penetrating gaze. His body oozed strength in the bulkiness of his frame and stance. She'd never realized how good the male human could look. Animals, flowers, mountains, and sunset were the pleasures of the world she'd known—the highlights of her life. But something about the way he gazed at her, in pure confidence, blessed peace, and sweet kindness, was richer and more compelling than anything she'd ever experienced.

"I mean it," she said, her voice barely above a whisper.

He cupped her cheeks between his palms. "I'm all yours."

She wanted to possess him for her own. Keep him with her always.

Ziana was right. She would start to feel human soon enough.

"Let's go." He winked at her then grabbed her two bags by the door.

She switched off her light and locked up behind her.

Their wedding ceremony progressed fast. They recited words about loving and caring for one another forever. Gelsey hated lying, knowing she wouldn't keep those promises. What reassured her was the knowledge Evan would forget her as soon as the fairy dust came upon his head. She would do him no harm. Yet, he swore forever to her. He could never fulfill the oath.

It didn't matter. She belonged in another world. Why else did her heart long for it every day? All these hours would be a dim memory when she went back home.

After buying a few snacks for the road, she climbed into Evan's pickup truck, and they began the journey.

"Where are you taking me?" she asked for the third time.

Evan just smiled at her and shrugged. "A surprise."

Her heart raced with the craziness of it. She knew she would enter nature away from the city, and the farther they went from the smog and concrete, the more at peace she felt. Yet, the unknown ahead of her caused her peace to erode away. Did other human females feel so afraid of having sex with a man? As far as she knew, the man wanted sex more than the woman many times. He was pumped with testosterone to keep the human race going. A woman had estrogen to make babies.

Unable to sleep even with the lulling effect of the car engine and the silence between them, she spent her time looking out the car window for birds, trees, and cows. Cows were one of her least favorite creatures, yet she felt for them. They were bred in mass for food. In many ways, the humans controlled the world. But they didn't know of the secret existence hidden from their eyes. Fairies weren't visible to them. At that very second, one of her friends could be perched on the roof of their vehicle, watching over her. She longed to be able to sense just one of them nearby.

"You're very quiet." Evan turned to her, taking his gaze off the road.

She shrugged. "Nothing much to say."

"We'll be there in about an hour." He smiled. "Why don't you read or listen to music? You brought nothing to amuse yourself with."

"When we get there, I'll take walks. I find the world around me amusement enough."

"You're a very visual person, then. Have you considered sketching or painting what you see?"

"Are you taking me to the Drakensberg Mountains? There're several hills and mountains surrounding us. I can smell the fresher air. Mmm, it's lovely." She sucked in a deep breath and her mood perked. It had been years since being assigned to the mountains and then only for a short stint. A mountain fairy spent the bulk of her life on the ranges, a savannah sprite in the bush. She'd flown over the snow-topped peaks in winter, awed by their majestic beauty, but didn't know them well.

"I think I made the right choice." He touched her knee and gave her a look that forced her to glance away. She wasn't used to someone caring for her so much. Sure, Marissa showed concern and so did her fairy friends and "mother," but they looked after many. This man seemed to care exclusively or predominantly for her. A part of her felt like she didn't deserve all this attention. No one deserved to be fussed over so much. Wouldn't it make one spoiled or self-centered?

"Cathedral Peak."

"I've heard of it."

"We're going to have the time of our lives."

She nodded, a measure of calm resting upon her, pushing away the increasing anxiety. Looking forward to something always helped take away some dread. Not all of it, but a little to balance it out. She smiled to herself. There she went again— always trying to harmonize nature. Maybe she hadn't lost her true self after all.

Sipping an alcoholic drink while watching the sun set helped calm Gelsey down a bit more. The stars appeared, and the air felt surprisingly cool for early summer. The mozzies had come out in full force, their wicked whine and persistent itch made sitting outside no longer pleasant.

Evan paid for the bill and put his wallet away.

The time had come. She bit her lip and took in a deep breath to calm herself. He had been good company, but they still had little in common. He worshipped her because of the fairy dust, not because he genuinely cared. She tried to tell herself that, but every time he looked into her eyes, she felt different. Tonight, she had to enter into a human rite of passage as required by the queen. Her heart hammered against her chest, and she couldn't work out whether fear or anticipation affected her.

"Our room is warmer. And so is my body." Evan tucked her against his side as they rose up from their seats outside the hotel restaurant.

She nodded and gave him a shaky smile.

They walked fast to their room while Evan led the way. She barely kept up with his step. He sure seemed in a hurry all of a sudden.

Once inside their room, she took off her shoes and wriggled her toes to stretch them then lay down on the bed, exhausted from a day with little activity but lots of change.

"I'm going to bathe. Will you join me?"

Gelsey nodded. She followed him into the bathroom, and as he ran the water, he removed his clothes. She took in his naked form—a strange need to scrutinize him overtaking her. His muscles were chiseled perfectly, rocks of strength molded against his body. She touched his upper arm muscle and giggled.

He spun her around and reached for the small buttons on the back of her dress, popping them open one at a time. The satin fabric sank to her feet. His hands ran down her back and onto the cheeks of her bottom, over the lacy underwear Marissa had insisted she wear today. It was a most uncomfortable garment that had dug into her crotch all day until she felt raw in her privates. She took the thong off but didn't turn around.

He gasped, running his fingers down her bare back. "You didn't wear a bra the whole day?"

"Is that a bad thing?"

"I wish I'd known."

"Why?"

"Maybe it was good I didn't know. The need to touch you would have been overwhelming. I couldn't have waited for us to be alone."

She turned to him while his warm hands swept over her bare abdomen. He tentatively caressed the skin above her breasts. Shudders ran through her. The breasts were for nourishing children, yet tonight, she longed for them to nourish her and Evan. Maybe this whole sex thing would be fun.

"Your nipples are pert and large."

"I thought every woman had the same. The water...."

Evan turned the taps off. "Come in."

She stepped into the warm bath and sat facing him. Evan's gaze remained fixed on her and swept over her form. His eyes looked wild, like an animal stalking its prey, yet soft as a mother dog with her puppies. Heat flooded her cheeks and washed over her. Did all the females feel warm and hungry at the same time being watched by the male humans? Fairies always felt familiar around one another.

She peered at him to gauge his response. He stared at her, his eyes strangely moist. Maybe he'd wet his face from the bath.

"I have never seen any woman like you."

Odd. Ziana had said she would be given the standard human form. The lumps on her back were almost invisible. Had he noticed them?

He lifted her chin with his fingers. "I mean in a good way. You're incredible."

"Thank you." She swallowed, more heat tingling throughout her body.

She understood what he meant. She'd seen many male humans, but none as beautiful as this man before her. His gaze was food for her soul, the vision of his body a memory she never wanted to let go. As he sat in the bath, his thigh muscles hid the private parts of him. She looked down at them, fascinated by the generosity of the male organs. The woman's lower parts seemed quite plain. The man displayed all to be seen. Boldly, she reached out to put her finger on his penis sticking up out of the water.

"Wait. Not yet."

Was it always so large? She hadn't noticed the size beneath the clothes. She wished she'd bothered more with her research about sex.

"Let me wash you."

How would it feel for his hands to touch her? She shivered, surprised because the water wasn't cold. "Okay."

He soaped a cloth from her toiletry bag until a rich lather formed. He began at her shoulders and worked downward, spending a little more time over her breasts. Every movement seemed deliberate and soft as a mother bird feeding her chicks. He eased her up. She stood with him as he soaped down her stomach, legs, and back. Emotion clogged her throat and warred with the dizzying sensations taking over her body. Why did his touch felt so good? She needed more. Strange tightening began in her pussy, the name humans gave to her female organ.

She took the cloth to clean it, not yet ready for him to touch, and he in turn cleaned himself quickly. While he washed, she admired the solid form of him, the growth of hairs on his chest, arms, and legs, like sprinkles of wild lavender on a field, ready for her to take a glorious whiff once dry and run her hands through them.

A strange compulsion overcame her. She couldn't hold herself away from him any longer. She gripped his arms while he still soaped the firm cheeks of his backside and pressed herself against him. The bubbles made their bodies slip and slide against one another. Gorgeous sensations engulfed every nerve while she wriggled against him. A cry escaped her lips just before she claimed his mouth with a gulp.

He reached for her breasts and rubbed them with smooth hands. When he touched the nipples with his fingertips, sweet peaks of sensation rippled through her. As his palm rubbed against them some more, tingles of pleasure flooded her—a feeling she'd never ever known, even as a fairy in the glen by a waterfall.

She arched her back, pushing her pelvis into his male organ. The hard rock pressed into her. He maneuvered himself to go inside her. This was it. At first, it hurt as the hard length of him eased into her only a little.

He sensed her pain and pulled out, continuing to rub her tits with his fingers. He tweaked them frantically, and she thought her body would flip over as though she almost lost all control yet also remained fully in the moment. Another cry came out of her mouth. She didn't care. She wanted more.

"Come to the bed. Dry yourself." He pulled away, and she moaned.

Before she could stop him, he padded toward the double bed in their suite.

She'd never dried herself so fast and almost ran to the bed. If this was sex, it felt amazing, better than a luxurious meal, than the first spring rains on her wings.

He lay on the bed, his naked form dry and flushed, his legs parted, and his gaze fixed on her. She enjoyed watching him study her from head to toe while she stood before him briefly. He rested the back of his head on his hands, making him appear deceptively relaxed. She knew his heart thudded as the pulse in his neck fluttered like crazy. His cock stood erect and swollen. What would it be like to have that within her properly? Would it feel as good as his fingers on her nipples? Somehow, she knew it would be just what she craved.

"Lie next to me. I want to explore you first."

"But...." She wanted to feel him enter her, for them to make the act of procreation although no babies yet. The drive to have the sexual act was very overwhelming in the human. Must be their survival mechanism. Yet, they'd bypassed procreation with their new technologies.

What would it be like to have his baby? She lay next to him but kept on pondering pregnancy. Evan and her having a child of their own—someone who looked like both of them yet a unique creature. She pushed the thought away. A fairy couldn't have kids with a human. Although she was human, she still had fairy blood. She'd turned into a hybrid.

His hands danced over her body again, bringing pure bliss to every nerve ending. At times, he touched her clumsily, but with patience, she prodded him away. Then he pushed his finger into her chasm.

"I don't want to penetrate you today. You're a virgin, aren't you?"

She nodded.

"It will hurt. I'm going to break through gently with my finger first. But let me play with your clit first."

This "clit" felt so good. At first, it prickled a little as he touched the sensitive part at the top of her lips. The sensation was too sharp—seeming to penetrate right into her, but after some gentle rubbing, a new rhythm began inside her, rising up to a higher crescendo than she'd ever known. With his other hand, he fiddled with her nipple. Her abdomen made strange squirming movements. It felt so much better to just let it take over. Rainbow lights shot across her vision, and her body became one with him and pure pleasure.

"Ah." She groaned as she jerked for some time and then stopped. "No more," she said, wishing for him to give her a rest. Warmth seeped to every extremity. Her hunger had been filled for now, sending peace throughout her body.

He gave her a drawn out kiss, his lips and tongue plump and wet. She enjoyed the contact even though her body felt spent.

"You can bring me to climax if you like," he said. "Rub my cock with your hands."

Realizing he needed some attention, too, she obliged, loving the tingly feeling when she touched his part.

"Here, hold me like this. And pump." He demonstrated with

his hand, his warm gaze upon her.

She grasped his shaft and imitated the action he'd indicated while she lay down next to him. Touching him felt so right, and her face nestled against his chest warmed her. His scent was heavenly, better than the sweetest herb or petal. She loved the hardness of his body—the opposite feel to hers. He projected power and vigor. As she pumped and pressed herself against him, wrapping her leg frantically around his, he groaned and became very large beneath her touch. Not long after rubbing his smooth and solid shaft, white liquid spurted from him into her hand and onto his stomach. Ah, the man's sperm. He stretched for something to clean up then eased back down on the bed with a big yawn.

"I tired you," she said, disappointed the sex was over.

"I'll be ready for more soon. I can't stay away from you for long." He gave a lazy grin.

As she looked into his eyes, she wanted to kiss him. This man had become so precious to her. He treated her with such care and tenderness and kept focused on her all the time.

He seemed to sense her need and, pressing his palms against the back of her head, brought her in for a kiss. After exploring each other's mouths in a delightful tangle of tongues, they embraced, and sleepiness came over her.

Every once in a while, she woke up with her head sweaty on his chest, his arms wrapped around her, and her thigh against his thick, warm leg. His skin upon hers felt so right as if they belonged together. She allowed herself to fall back to sleep. They would dress later.

Chapter Six

Gelsey woke as the first bird chirped outside their window, surprised to find herself covered. Evan lay next to her in the dark, moonlight splashed on his fringed brow. He looked so dear, so peaceful. They'd woken in the night, and he'd penetrated her for the first time. Without pain. His fullness inside of her had been the climax of their time together—so intense had the pleasure and intimacy been. She wanted many more of these moments with him.

They had a year. Would it be long enough?

She sprung upright with a start. Her heart raced in her throat. No way would she stay in the human world, no matter what temptations sought to hold her back. Nothing would distract her from reaching her dream. She would never fit in as a woman totally. The human world was harsh, lonely, and scary.

"Gelsey?" Evan sat up and touched her lightly on the stomach.

"I had a bad dream." She had sort of—she'd dreamed she lost her gold fairy dust but had found it inside one of her suitcase compartments.

He wrapped his arms around her. "Sorry."

His deep voice splashed warmth over her soul, and she lay back, glad he'd woken. She didn't feel so alone anymore.

He chatted for some time, giving suggestions of what they

would do once the sun came up. "Well, I think a good breakfast and a hike in the mountains is in order. We'll find the bushman paintings."

"I'd like that."

Light seeped through the curtains. More birds began their songs. One of the greatest of fairy sorrows was the disintegration of the Koi-San—bushman—people. They were in touch with nature and knew how to make use of what the earth had to offer. They didn't over-exploit the environment but worked with it. The bushmen were the humans most like the animals—fully balanced with the eco-system. But the Dutch, English, and Zulu people had killed many of the Koi-San as they came into South Africa centuries ago. The bushmen didn't have the warring spirit to fight them. Several still existed, but their tribes were almost obsolete. One day, years back, Gelsey had relished the privilege of watching a tribe in the Kalahari. She couldn't wait to see their paintings.

Evan sat up, a mischievous twinkle in his eye, and pulled the cover down to study her naked form. The awkwardness had faded somewhat. She enjoyed the hunger in his gaze when he perused her breasts and feminine parts.

"What a feast for the eyes so early in the morning. Better than any sunrise."

She smiled wide. "Shall we watch the sunrise together?"

"Can we fit in some sex beforehand?"

Gelsey rose and pulled back the curtain. The horizon looked a dark gray. "We have about twelve and a half minutes before the sun comes up."

Evan laughed. "Very precise prediction. Your observation of things amazes me."

"Wait until we go on our hike." She turned back and gave him a cheeky grin.

"I can't wait."

"Do you enjoy helping the environment?" She sat down on the bed opposite him.

"Hush." He placed his finger over her lips. "We'll talk later."

He reached to kiss her. At first, weariness encompassed her. They'd kissed and fondled so much the night before, but after his tongue teased hers a few times, fire shot into her and stirred up the longings she didn't know could erupt so quickly again. Within seconds, they writhed on the bed together, their bodies intertwined in sweet closeness and heat. His heart beat against her chest, his manliness hard against her pelvis.

"Evan...." She moaned his name.

"Sweet Gelsey." His echoing cry pierced something in her soul as if she were his savior, his very nourishment.

She lay down on her back, and he hovered over her. The look of passion in his eyes took her breath away. She'd never seen him so handsome before. Sex did this to humans. The strongest magic in their world seemed to be the love between a man and woman. To think, she'd always believed humans were uncaring creatures.

With a delighted expression on his face, he slid his arousal into her vagina still sensitive from the night before. At first, his cock rubbed a little roughly against her, but as his arms wrapped around her and he sucked her nipples, moisture lubricated her channel. His organ slid in and out of her in glorious sweetness, sending pleasure through her body, each wave more intense than the last. She pressed her pelvis in rhythmic arches toward him, clinging to his back, so wanting more and more. Within moments, they rode a surge of pure ecstasy together.

Finished, he rested on her and sighed. "You're amazing."

She gasped for breath.

"I'm sorry. I forget I'm a heavy man and you're a little elf."

She laughed. A magic creature she was. What would he think if he knew? Hate her for lying to him? Be nauseated by her?

She pushed the invading thoughts away.

He lay next to her and took her hand. "I've never felt this way before," he said, nuzzling her neck with his nose.

She snuggled up to him, her core still throbbing with the glorious climax. "Me neither."

"I've been with other women before."

White-hot jealousy streaked through her. She was unable to speak.

"It's different between us. Alive, real. There's a connection I've never felt before. When I look in your eyes, I know I will always want to be with you. And the feeling grows every minute."

Her breath hitched, and tears came to her eyes. Too bad his feelings were the effects of the fairy dust.

"I've heard about people meeting their soul mates or partners who they just belong to. I always thought the idea too fanciful. I thought you had to work to make things click. I do believe it requires some work, but with you, it's been easy and natural, like breathing."

"It's wonderful, Evan." She squeezed his hand.

He swiped a tear away from beneath her eye. "Don't cry."

She turned away, holding in the sobs.

He held her while she cried into her pillow, caressing her with such love. This man had chiseled a place in her soul. When she left for home, she might be able to forget him in her mind, but would her heart ever forget him?

"Why are you crying?" He stroked her hair, sending sweet shivers through her.

She rolled over to face him. "I'm so overwhelmed. I've never had a man care so much for me before."

The smile lighting his face wiped away the concerned frown.

Her sobs subsided, and she glanced up at the ceiling then studied the earthy pieces and soft furnishings of the resort. They'd harmonized the look very well. Humans were talented at blending colors and shapes together to create an atmosphere. The room had a definite African feel. Although she'd only ever lived in Africa, the vibe of the continent had been entrenched in her—the deep, rich browns, reds, and greens, the ruggedness and yet a simple, undeniable beauty the African savannah and bush held. This room captured it perfectly. The mountain air from outside breezed in through the windows, billowing the curtains in a dance. Joy rose up within her.

She began to hum softly as he lay down beside her again—a song in harmony with the bird noises outside. He remained silent while stroking her arm. The music calmed her, and after she'd sung for ages, she arose to wash.

"That was magical. I've never felt so calm in all my life," he called to her from the bed while she wet her hair and washed her face.

"Really?"

"You have a gift."

"What do you mean?" She peered around the bathroom door, her towel on her dampened head.

"You have a calming influence. You'd make a marvelous mother. We wouldn't have any colicky babies."

She disappeared back into the bathroom before he could see the look of horror she felt on her face. Did Evan want children? So soon?

"Don't panic." He laughed as he came through to join her in the bathroom, grabbing his toothbrush. She admired his naked form once again. Would she ever grow tired of it?

"I don't want children yet. Not for a while. We haven't discussed the subject actually. I hope you don't have strong alternate ideas."

"I hadn't thought," she lied.

"Good. We don't even need to think about it yet. We're still young, still discovering each other."

"I agree." She let out a breath. *Whew!* Imagine if he started pressuring her to have a child. Seemed like he was one of the humans keen on children, but the fact he wanted to wait and didn't want to let nature take its course, showed the modern influence.

"Did you take precautions?" He came up behind her, and she saw them both in the mirror. A strange feeling to see them together. They looked like a couple—like they belonged with each other.

"I'm on the pill."

"Good. You were sensible."

She turned from their reflections, so intense was the sense of oneness and his loving words. She finished washing her face and proceeded to brush her teeth. Her commission had turned out to be the craziest thing ever. But Ziana was right. Her life before had dimmed a little in her memory. She felt all ready to go on her adventure. Something had changed since last night—she'd become the most privileged of all fairies. She'd experienced human love.

cs

"Oh, no!" Marissa gaped at her as she walked into the florist three days later.

"What?" Gelsey shrugged. Maybe something bad had happened at the shop. Or did her hair look funny? She'd taken less care in her appearance this morning because Evan had distracted her by kissing the back of her neck while she sat in the front of her dressing table's oval mirror. He'd bought one and set it up for her in their new bedroom. The kissing on her neck had led to kissing on the mouth, then grappling of.... The list could go on, but Marissa stared at her while all she could think about....

"You've had good sex the last few days."

"I beg your pardon?" Had Evan told her something? Had Marissa sent someone to spy on them?

"It's all over your face. You have a drugged, lovesick look."

"Oh, you can tell?"

Marissa laughed. "Don't deny it, and don't get too Cheshire cat satisfied. It doesn't stay good. You'll have kids one day and get old and your bodies will be tired. Believe me, I know it. And the romance doesn't last either."

"I assume you speak for everyone?"

"I can't speak for everyone." She turned away, her voice high-and defensive. "But I think I do."

"Well, not good news at all." Gelsey pulled some dried stems out of a pot and dusted the vase with a cloth. "I thought it would last forever."

Marissa sighed. "I'm too cynical. Don't listen to me. But when you have kids, it does change things. That I know for sure. Even getting back from the honeymoon to real life and work pressures dims things a bit. I don't mean it's all bad but...well, I'll stop here."

"I need to know these things. Thanks for being honest with me." She needed to know them for more reasons than the other woman could ever know.

"You're so good." Marissa straightened out some ornaments on a shelf and joined Gelsey in the cleaning. "This place picks up dust way too fast."

"I'm good?"

"You're just so innocent and accepting. I wish I had a bit of your freshness."

Gelsey shrugged. Sometimes she wished everything wasn't so confusing and unknown in the human world.

"Well, how was the honeymoon anyway? Where did you go?"

"Cathedral Peak."

"It's beautiful there. Chris took me there years ago before we divorced."

"We went on a hike every day."

"There are lots of walks in the area, but it can get tiring."

"We took it slow and discussed the bird life and plants a lot." Her knowledge of the flora and small creatures had fascinated Evan. She'd had to come up with the story that she'd studied botany and zoology. He'd believed her and asked why she hadn't found a more substantial job than a florist. Unable to come up with a plausible lie to explain her current position, she'd changed the subject, and thankfully, they'd reached a small waterfall and became enamored with the cool water.

Evan spent a large portion of his time behind the camera much to Gelsey's dismay. No one could enjoy the beauty of things behind a tiny screen. Tonight, Evan would show her the photos. He said it would all be worth it. Really? She liked to not only see nature, but smell, feel, and sense it around her. Trapped behind the device broke the contact.

"You're in another world." Marissa changed the window display, adding in some new dry arrangements she'd made while Gelsey was away.

"Just thinking how much I despise people taking pictures of everything instead of just enjoying the experience."

Marissa laughed. "It's called memories."

She nodded, wondering what could explain the sudden ache in her gut. *Memories. What for? They would be forgotten soon enough.*

Suddenly, the year looming ahead of her didn't seem very long at all.

Evan walked through the store doorway.

"I thought you needed to be at work," she said, trying to hide the flutter of excitement at seeing him earlier than she'd expected.

"I stopped by briefly to ask you a few things." He smiled wide. "Or maybe I was missing you a bit." He gave a lingering, warm kiss on her cheek, and she grasped his hand as though it was a life source.

Marissa rolled her eyes. "It's just been an hour since you saw each other. I've got some stuff to do in the back."

"Don't go." Gelsey half meant it. If her friend couldn't deal with their love, what to do? Obviously, human love was so intense that if one didn't have it, it hurt. Yet, most of the time, Marissa seemed a happy person. She survived without it. The thought assured Gelsey she would more than survive once she returned to her friends and lived out in the sunshine and fresh air every day. She faced her husband. "What did you want to ask?"

"I only have two clients today, so I'm going to use the extra time to clear out your home and bring your stuff over to my place. Is that okay? I don't want to just take over, but once it's done, we can relax together tonight. Of course, it might take more than two days if you have lots of things."

"I don't have much." Her hands shook a little, so she wiped

the counter clean with a damp cloth to remove remnants of dry grasses and to calm her down. Marissa must have been too busy the last few days to clean up properly.

"Interesting." He gave her a knowing look. What could he think about her having few possessions? That she just led a simple life? He couldn't work out she'd lived in this world for a month and hadn't gathered much stuff yet. It seemed humans gathered many things they didn't even use. They were like squirrels, hiding things for the winter months but many didn't know the true feeling of scarcity.

"I will need your key, then." He touched her hand and a spark shot through her.

"Sure." She fumbled in her handbag under the counter for her house key and handed it to him.

"Have you phoned the agent yet to organize the termination of your lease? And the municipality to disconnect your electricity and water?"

She shook her head. "I've only been at work for less than an hour."

He touched her arm. "No pressure. Just don't want you to spend money unnecessarily."

"I know." Another side of the human world she found very complicated—dealing with money. Ziana had set up her home and electricity and water connections. She'd temporarily entered the realm for her and had gotten her settled in a job and home very fast. At least Evan seemed to know these things way better than she did, but she hated the feeling of not being in control. Just a year, she told herself. Back at home, she could direct her life, although, if she received her promotion, she would be out of her league big time. But in a good way. Excitement threaded through her. Yes, the wonderful honeymoon hadn't dulled her true purpose. For a moment, she'd let the drugged effect of love lull her into thinking this life might be for her. As Marissa had said, the feeling wouldn't last. By the end of the year, she'd probably be hankering to get out of her prison.

"You look far away again." Evan prodded her arm. "Okay?"

"Yes, yes of course."

"Great. I'll see you later."

"Don't worry about cooking supper. I'll think of something," she said to him, sensing she'd shown no gratefulness after the kind assistance he'd offered and that she'd possibly hurt his feelings. "I'm sure you'll be tired after moving all my stuff."

"Okay." He winked at her, calming some of her harried thoughts.

She'd deal with the confusion later when her year ended. The only thing she really needed to do was put her all into this human thing and live and feel it to the best of her ability.

൧

Evan unlocked the door to Gelsey's little simplex in the group of homes she lived in. The sound of the key turning as he locked it behind him and the placing of the cardboard boxes and tape dispenser on the tile floor echoed in the open-plan lounge, dining room, and kitchen. A simple coach and TV on a stand stood like a sentry in the corner of the room that appeared deceptively large. He couldn't find a bookshelf or ornaments, but at least there were several houseplants breaking the monotony of the décor. He headed for the kitchen. He hated packing dishware and pans and figured if he did them first, the rest would be a breeze.

Opening the cupboards, he gaped at the vast emptiness. This woman looked like she just holidayed here and didn't reside in Newcastle. Tiny, creepy little tendrils of fear and doubt took grasp of the compartments of his brain. Had she planned on staying here short term? As far as he knew, she'd only been at the florist for a month. Or was she running from something? Had she been in jail? He'd married her with a total sense of certainty that she was the woman for him, but suddenly he wasn't so sure he'd made the right choice. Not because of her character and not because he doubted the love he had for her, but because of the strangeness of her circumstances.

It took ninety minutes to pack up her whole home. He surveyed the empty space, six boxes at his feet, and sighed. He had to confront her tonight. Needed answers. He rubbed his head. Had infatuation and love made him lose all sense?

He packed the boxes into the back of his truck and drove home. While he made space in his cupboards for her belongings, memories of his time with Gelsey wafted like the aroma of fresh pizza over his mind, clearing away most of the fear. She was as pure as they came. She could never have run away from the police or done anything bad. Her silky nightdress lay in a heap on the floor next to their unmade bed, reminding him of their early-morning lovemaking, this time slow and savored. He picked the garment up and breathed in her scent—warm and sweet. He could almost feel her hair against his nose and mouth, taste her sweet arousal although he hadn't licked her pussy yet. He had moved slowly with her although she seemed comfortable with everything they'd done together so far.

His heart raced with anticipation for the night ahead. He would arouse her with his tongue and taste her cream he'd smelled many times in their moments together.

Despite the doubts, he wouldn't talk to her. She would bring up her past when ready. There were secrets there—he could tell by the way she sometimes went into another world far away— her eyes almost glazed over with...what? Longing, sad memories, or pain? He couldn't tell. He wanted to soothe whatever caused her to switch off sometimes but chose not to ask about it until she opened up. He had his own pain and hadn't shared it with many. Maybe the past was coming back to haunt him. Maybe Gelsey would disappear one day and never come back. His throat tightened, and he took some deep breaths to ease the panic. He'd lost something dear once before—left without a trace. What if it happened again?

She didn't seem to have put roots down here. Would she leave at the hint of any difficulty? Although she acted innocent and sweet, she could surprise him.

He dropped the silken nightdress into the cupboard and

carried the boxes to the various rooms where they would be unpacked. He'd never realized how long he'd hungered for a woman to share his home. It felt right to him. His heart felt full and complete. Confronting and pushing her away wouldn't calm the fears inside of him. Maybe the anxiety was unfounded, based on past hurt. Once he'd neatened up their bedroom and put all her belongings away, he drove to a client's house to complete an installation he'd begun the day before—three solar panels and a geyser.

Energy and zeal pulsed through him. Gelsey's obvious passion for the environment made him feel more certain his profession was needed. She had so many ideas and had shared them with him on their hikes in the Drakensberg. He could glean from her ideas. How could he have doubted her?

He had it bad. Love had hit him stronger than he'd ever expected. Even his mom had said she didn't think he would ever get his heart broken again because he'd learned to play it safe. He was calculated, reserved, and very cautious. What Gelsey had done to him should be deemed nothing short of a miracle.

Whatever happened, they would get through it together.

Chapter Seven

*G*elsey wrapped the knitted shawl around her shoulders, but it did nothing to ward off the autumn chill. Fairies didn't enjoy cold weather, but somehow, as a human stuck inside, the cold seemed to seep into her bones—and winter hadn't arrived yet.

"I'm going for a walk. It's lunch hour," she told Marissa.

Her boss nodded and went back to the books. Poor Marissa, trying to make ends meet when there weren't any special occasions lined up to produce prolific flower sales. Although the funerals had been sparse, much to her relief, it didn't do well for their little shop. Gelsey needed to brainstorm ideas for the shop. She'd brought in some new flower arrangement ideas because of her keen knowledge of indigenous flowers, but those alone hadn't increased sales enough.

"What about fairy ornaments?" She spoke to herself while she walked down the busy street, the gray concrete pavements matching the dull gray of the clouds. Fairy-themed cards, fairy-wing arrangements. She smiled as the ideas kept coming and wondered what Marissa would think. She'd laugh and dismiss them.

Her new ideas did little to break through the darkness of her mood. It had nothing to do with the shop. Yes, Marissa's concern weighed upon her at times, but Gelsey was well aware of the balance of life and how difficulties always led to good times. She'd learnt from her fairyhood that droughts may cause death and scarcity, but soon the rains would come. The ground would soak up the refreshment and the plants would flourish the next luscious spring, more than they had in years. Trials often led to prosperity.

No, her mood resulted from her marriage. As much as Evan remained enamored with her, he'd withdrawn over the last few weeks. A constant ache bloomed like an unwanted weed in her heart. It stayed with her no matter what she did or where she went. She'd become dependent on him being taken with her body and mind.

Since they'd married, almost every night they'd shared a passion that surprised and drew Gelsey into its intensity. Then they'd talked for hours—Evan sharing his childhood, all his business ideas and dreams, and Gelsey laughing and cheering him on. She'd met his parents and loved them.

Somehow, she'd deflected too much talk about herself, concocting up a simple childhood in a small rural town in Northern Zululand. She knew the area well because she'd spent a long assignment there helping out the insects and small rodents in the foresters' tree plantations. So, in a sense, a part of her childhood had been there—where she'd first started working as an eco-balance fairy.

Some days, she considered asking Marissa what could be wrong. But the woman would just say the problems in her marriage were normal. Gelsey didn't want it to be normal. She wanted everything back to how they'd been when first married. Was he growing tired of her? Did he love someone else? Surely not. She had no idea how to tell. All she knew was men found others in the human world. So did women. The thought scared her more than anything else.

To ask him would be even more difficult. He'd worked late almost every night the last few weeks. He came home exhausted and not very talkative.

Gelsey walked into the town central library to find some

books on marriage. Maybe she needed an education because the distance growing between them couldn't go on.

She sat down at one of the study tables in the children's section, armed with several thick books. She had twenty minutes to find a way to ease the huge gaping hole in her heart and the swirling dread in the pit of her stomach, which grew bigger with each passing minute.

Ω

"I've just got one more installation tonight then I'll spend time with you tomorrow. It's Sunday. No one wants to do installations then."

The last words Evan had spoken to her the night before kept replaying like an irritating rap song on the radio. He'd come home so late, she'd fallen asleep before seeing him, his supper drying out in the warming drawer in the kitchen. As much as the marriage books had helped her see things in perspective, the hurt remained.

Yes, men got busy. They had a big burden to carry financially. Gelsey had increased the burden by moving in with him, and her florist's salary wasn't much. She'd lived very simply her first month in the human world before Evan had married her. Since then, she'd known luxury and been spoiled. Had he begun to resent her?

She'd read in one of the books that men often closed up when they were burdened. Maybe he felt overwhelmed. But it still annoyed her that he wouldn't give her an inkling of what was wrong.

What was she to do if he didn't even talk to her?

While the birds woke up and sang brightly, Evan lay fast asleep next to her. What time had he gotten in? Did his clients like him working so late? Doubt seared through her.

Tears filled her eyes. She hadn't cried much since entering the human world—just once during their honeymoon when the force of Evan's love had first entered her being. Her throat ached with holding back the gush of tears. She hated feeling so vulnerable and so dependent on one person's attention. Maybe this love thing wasn't so great after all.

Evan opened his eyes just as she reached for something to blow her nose. He gazed right at her as if he knew.

Taking in a breath, he spoke, his eyes big and face wide-awake. "What's wrong?"

At the concern in his gaze and his gentle touch on her arm, sobs took over.

He hugged her close. "What's happened?" He spoke low into her ear.

She pulled away and inhaled a deep breath, bracing herself for letting it all out. "It's us. What's wrong? Why don't we talk? You're always busy. I keep thinking you don't love me anymore." She covered her wobbling mouth with her hand.

He sighed and rubbed his head as if it ached. A stiff silence stood between them. Had she made him furious? Maybe the love between them wasn't strong.

"I'm so careless." His voice was tight. "I should have told you. I didn't want to worry you, but I've had some problems with the business. Some important clients haven't paid for their installations, and my supplier refused to ship to me because of relationship problems. He won't budge, no matter what I say."

"Why didn't you tell me? What have you been doing every night?"

"I've been investigating another supplier but no luck." He sighed, anguish filling his face, deeper furrows forming on his forehead. "I'm selling the business."

Gelsey couldn't believe it and recognized panic in his eyes. If she showed shock, it would make him feel worse. Why hadn't she noticed something seriously wrong on his side? Instead, she'd worried about her own needs not being met. Everything in her craved to soothe him.

"You're not worried?" He gazed into her eyes.

She shrugged. "Something I believe about life—it comes in seasons. You have winter and summer, bad times and good, but you always make it through."

His eyes darkened, and he sucked in a breath. "I can vouch for that, but sometimes the cold of winter still stays in your heart."

Gelsey felt such love for him she wanted to wipe away all the pain. "What happened, Evan?"

"I never told you about Trish, did I?"

"Trish?" Her pulse raced as she questioned who he meant and what it would mean for their relationship, but she kept eye contact with him. Today was about him and his needs. "Who's she?"

"She's not alive anymore. She died when I was a kid. My twin sister."

"Oh." Gelsey had lost a few fairy friends but didn't understand Evan's pain too well. Although, if she had to lose him....

"We did everything together. I was never the same again. Took me years to get my passion for life back. In fact, *you've* given it back to me." His eyes teared, and he fisted the top of the duvet cover. "Do you know what it's like to lose your best friend, the light of your life?"

Gelsey shook her head. Her throat tightened as she read the pain in his features. She'd never experienced the measure of agony she saw in his eyes—and didn't want to. "I can't imagine...."

He stroked her hand. "She'll always be in my memories. Just wish I could remember more." He went quiet but held her hand as if it were a life source.

A melody entered her soul and came out her mouth instinctively. She hummed in harmony with the birds, twining his fingers with hers, the song taking over her soul.

He lay back on the bed and closed his eyes as if in a trance. She smiled. She'd made use of the one fairy power she hadn't lost. Ziana had told her.... There were many things she didn't understand about what Ziana had said. If only she could speak to her. No, Evan needed her at present. Her questions could wait.

After humming for some time while the sun came up and the bird song increased, Gelsey lay next to her husband on her side. He grasped her against him so they were tucked into each other.

"You wipe it all away. I love you," he said.

The ache inside her eased, and she dozed off, at peace with her world.

l&#x8;

Gelsey's heart hammered so hard her chest ached. Evan jumped up and down at the foot of the bed, his arms in the air, shouting at the top of his lungs.

She'd gone from a deep sleep to hysteria, and her heart didn't want to ease in its race. *What?* Had something bad happened?

"I've got it."

At last, his words made sense. Well, sort of. "Got what?"

"The answer."

"The answer?"

He laughed and stopped jumping to sit at the foot of the bed, taking hold of her toes under the covers. She wriggled them in response to his touch. Intimacy with him never bored her.

"What to do about my business."

"Oh." A smile came, and from the corner of her eye, she could tell they had slept late into the middle of the morning. There had been many sleepless and restless nights for both of them. So unfairy-like. She'd always woken up with the birds. All fairies did.

"I'm going to make the solar panels myself."

"Really? Isn't that hard?"

"I know what components and wiring go into them. I know where to get the raw materials. I have contacts, but the hardest part is setting up a small factory."

"Could be difficult."

He slapped her on the leg, enthusiasm brimming from his

gaze. "I like a challenge."

She smiled again. That's one thing they had in common.

"My office is next to a small plastics supplier. They have a 'for sale' sign on their window—been there for weeks. I'm going to expand my office and add a warehouse. It's all coming to me now. Everything lay before me, waiting for me to grab up the opportunity." He sighed and gazed at her, his navy eyes the bottom of a luxurious pool, swirling with emotion and strength. "Do you believe in fate?"

"What do you mean?"

"Do you believe sometimes life, or maybe even God, orchestrates things for us that are beyond our control, just to help us along the way?"

"I never have. I've always believed we have to do what we can to make things happen." Affecting the world was the basis of fairy magic. She did sometimes wonder how the earth seemed to keep going despite the way it had been abused. Why sometimes, the creatures she'd attended to had survived against the most difficult odds. She also wondered why Evan had walked into the florist on the day when she was desperate to fulfill her commission. If it had been someone else, would she feel the same way for him?

"You did it."

"I did what?" Her breath caught. Did he know she'd sprinkled the fairy dust on him?

"You calmed me and lulled me to sleep. Something happened when you hummed with the birds. I love you, Gelsey. I will never ever love anyone like you. There's some powerful magic between us, and I never want it to die."

She blinked, mixed emotions rising within. Never ever love someone like her? If she left in seven months, how would he feel? She had to know for sure he would never remember anything from their time together because she could never turn away from him then. Staring into his merry eyes, she wanted to hold onto the closeness they shared forever. It would not be possible. She couldn't stay here. She wasn't even allowed to. The magic between them would die. The fairy dust worked for a year. After the magic faded, Evan wouldn't love her anymore.

There. In just over half a year, she would depart—the best for both of them.

Evan climbed up next to her and took her face in his hands, kissing her roughly on the lips. Fervent longing took over. They hadn't made love in days, and the hunger within her raged like a fire lapping up the forest. She slid her hands down his T-shirt, the friction of his chest hairs rough against her palms. He groaned as she skimmed past his nipples.

He ran burning fingers on her buds through the nightdress and the smoothness of the silk made her soar into ecstasy.

"It will be over for me far too soon," she said, her voice broken.

He pulled away. "Then I'll tease you instead."

She groaned and rolled her eyes at him, but the wicked grin he gave sent her stomach into flips and spins.

He peeled off the layers of clothing he wore. Removing his clothes took her to a new level she hadn't reached without climaxing before. She'd so missed seeing him bare and pure, like the wild countryside not hemmed in by fences and orderliness.

"You're incredible," she said, touching his cheek, his chest, the dip by his pelvis, and then ending by his raised arousal. She stroked his rod, the fullness taking her back to the memories of all their adventures together. How could the last five months of marriage have gone by so fast? It seemed like sex got better the more they knew each other, the more practice they had.

"Today, I want to tease you with my tongue."

"Okay." She'd pushed him away from doing it many times, thinking it couldn't be nice for him, but today she wanted to try it.

"Lie down and open your legs."

She obeyed, a smile staying and not wanting to leave.

At first, he stroked her near her hips, on her stomach, and above the arch of her soft, curly hairs. She sighed as goose bumps flooded her being. Then he buried his face into her crevice and pressed his tongue between her lips. She gasped at the sharp sensation.

He continued despite her clamping with hesitation. She'd become used to him entering her many times, fondling her breasts, and even needling her buttocks, but this idea seem foreign. She'd never considered humans enjoyed tasting the bodily fluids of one another.

Oh! What was that? His tongue formed a powerful tool able to bring sensations she never thought possible. She groaned and arched toward the glorious sensation.

Holding back as much as possible, she didn't climax right away but cringed when liquid gushed from her pussy onto his face.

"I'm sorry," she said.

"It's so sexy." He continued, unfazed by her reticence. His unlimited desire for her only heightened the spasms shooting through her body. Unable to control the power surging through her, she gripped onto the sheet with her fists so she didn't crush his face. Groaning, she allowed his touch to send her to another perfect world. Within minutes, she was spent and warmth seeped through every extremity of her being. Joy danced within her.

Evan came up and kissed her. She received his cock inside her where it truly belonged. As he pushed upon her, he gazed at her, hunger and love blazoned upon his gaze. His love seared her soul, and she blinked back tears. Her body responded once again, and the waves of orgasm took over. He laid on top of her for some time, the beat of their hearts as one, yet two separate entities.

What a wonderful feeling to be one again. She'd so missed his closeness and the magic they shared.

Evan fell asleep again next to her, but she lay on the bed, wide-awake. Had she really helped him to calm down? This gift couldn't be taken lightly. He believed in fate. A force that made things happen outside of oneself. If fate had brought them together, why were they destined to part? Darkness descended upon her mind. The peace from earlier fled, and a war began in her heart. She grasped his hand, wishing his closeness might somehow ease the confusion, but nothing could take away the question burning within her. How would she leave him at the end of the year? Yet, how could she not?

Chapter Eight

"What is the problem?" Marissa never raised her voice at her, but Gelsey deserved it this time.

"I can't talk about it."

"Yeah, it's been nearly five months of marriage. To be expected."

She shook her head. Yes, her moods had been terrible as of late, but not because she was tired of Evan. Was it possible to feel such immense joy and sorrow at the same time? The last few weeks, she'd been spending all her free time working with him in kitting out his new factory. They'd supervised a team of painters to peel off the horrible chipped gray paint on the walls and layer a new sunny yellow in a glossy finish. The room looked so much brighter already. She'd helped him choose tiles for the floors and even nailed in new shelves for his raw materials. They'd worked together late into the night, but the lack of sleep hadn't affected her. Doing things together invigorated her. Evan never failed to make her feel like a part of his body—like his other self. He confided everything in her—every decision, every thought. Her courage to question the strain between them had only revealed how much a part of his life she wanted to be. She cared about what he did every day, how his business was going, and the extent of the burdens he carried in providing for them.

But she found it impossible to put her whole heart into their relationship when she knew "they" would be over within several months. The questions poured in while she worked. Sometimes, she didn't want to be alone anymore. She used to love walks in the garden at their home. She hadn't gone on one in weeks because every time she did, she was reminded of her other life and the pull to go back to her fairy home, yet the horror of breaking the bond with Evan.

"I've never known you to refuse to do a funeral arrangement." Marissa worked furiously, placing michi daisies, red gerberas, pink chrysanthemums, white St Joseph lilies, and greenery in an oasis shaped like a cross.

"The person died unnecessarily."

"When are you going to realize you work at a florist shop and not a hospital? We don't prevent deaths, we make the honoring of the person lost more special and easier to handle."

"We don't do enough weddings anymore. Why don't people get married?"

Marissa laughed. "People hook up and live together nowadays. Your setup was quite unusual. Where have you been, girl? You're as naïve as they come. I would think you came from another dimension or time period."

Heat rose up her neck and pulsed on her cheeks. "Um...."

"Just kidding. I like your fresh take on things. Were you homeschooled?"

"What's that?"

Marissa rolled her eyes. "Well, at least you're pretty brilliant at arranging flowers. I would be lost without you."

"Really? Thanks. Let me finish the arrangement." She took the flowers from her and placed them into the foam block. She imagined the arrangement was for a wedding this time, and inspiration took over. She'd never learned to deal with death too well, even as a fairy. Actually, death had made more sense then, before she'd experienced human love. In this world, she saw it as separation.

"Great. Then I can do some admin work."

"Just wait." She help up her hand as if to say stop. "This living together thing, does it work better than marriage?"

"Not sure. Never been one for statistics. Why do you ask?"

"Do people have kids when they live together?"

"Any couple who sleeps together can have kids."

"I know that. I'm not so stupid."

"Well, most of my friends who lived together got married if they wanted kids. When they were pretty serious about the relationship and knew it would work long term."

"What makes them sure?"

She laughed, grabbing a file from the filing cabinet. "Now there's a million-dollar question we'd all love to know the answer to."

"True. Sorry, about the twenty questions."

"You're a sweetie, Gelsey. Something about your honesty and curiosity makes life seem so much less serious."

"I'm glad."

"I've got to get stuck in and finish the accounts and tax stuff. I'll be in the back room."

"Sure."

Gelsey finished the arrangement with some greenery and clipped off a few excess leaves. She called the delivery driver and asked him to take it to a home in the Signal Hill area, the suburb up the steep hill looking down over the whole of Newcastle. She set to work on a group of arrangements for a conference, but her mind was working overtime.

Ziana had given her an option to meet with her—but only in an emergency. An emergency would be if her or her husband's life was in danger, or if the magic wasn't working anymore. Yet, the questions boiling inside of her caused her to falter. She couldn't go on like this—she'd reached breaking point. She struggled to sleep at night, was irritable with everyone, even Evan, and would drop into times of severe depression and confusion and forget her whereabouts and what her life was about.

No one would understand her confusion. No human could

help her. Not a soul would believe her story.

For her to complete the commission and be a wife to Evan, she needed help. This constituted an emergency. Tomorrow, she would take off early and meet Ziana on the spot up on Signal Hill—a little place tucked away in a small overgrown area, far from humanity—where she had been shown a portal to her home when life had been carefree. Where she'd never known the pain that came with the fear of separation.

How she would get through the next twenty-four hours, she didn't know.

છ

Evan drew the tea bag several times until Gelsey's drink turned a dark orange, almost brown color. He opened a packet of Eet Sum Mors—her favorite shop-bought shortbread biscuit—and set several on a plate, with a few autumn leaves to the side. His wife was crazy about the outdoors, and even a few leaves would light up her face. The ones he'd chosen covered the full spectrum of fall colors—dark green, yellow, orange, burgundy, and lastly brown. She'd taught him to think in all this detail. He couldn't help smiling, but the grin fled, replaced by a sucked-in breath.

His simple treats for her did little to dispel the despair creeping into his soul. What was eating away at her? She hadn't gone outside in weeks, keeping herself buried in a book or numbly watching TV, a pastime she'd despised when they first married. Her face looked deathly pale. Gelsey had always had good color—a peaches-and-cream, or British, complexion with soft skin and ruddy cheeks. Her pallor had changed to a pasty yellow with dark rings under her eyes. Sure, it was late autumn and the cold weather had set in, but surely that hadn't caused such morose and strange behavior.

He stirred the tea again, gathering the courage to face her. She tended to irritability, but not severe. He loved her for being so patient, even though he could tell she was carrying something very deep and painful. He was never one to pry, but this couldn't go on. Her suffering had become his own. She wasn't sleeping at night. He would often wake up and find her out the bed, pacing the passage or leafing through boring books like a set of dusty, old encyclopedias his parents had given to him from his school days.

He found her dozing on the couch with the TV on a low hum, flickering light through the darkened room. Although the sun hadn't fully set, the curtains were drawn and no lamp put on.

Would they get through this?

"Here's something for you. Your favorite vanilla chai tea and Eet Sum Mors." He set the tray down on the coffee table. She opened her eyes and smiled, but it didn't reach her eyes.

"Thank you." She sat up as though it took every ounce of effort. Taking a sip of tea, she stared at the TV, a blank look on her face.

"That's it. I can't take it anymore. What the blazers is the problem? You were upset with me for not sharing what was bothering me, but you mope about like a half-human, unable to enjoy anything. Is it the business challenges? Did I involve you too much? Did I tire you out?"

Gelsey's eyes went wide as though she hadn't expected him to notice how crazy she'd been acting.

"No, it's nothing."

"There is something. Don't hold your heart away from me. We've decided to be open with one another, to share everything."

She stared at him, her mouth poised as if she would speak. Her eyes held pain, deep pain, and he longed to delve the mystery of her. Somehow, he knew the revelation wasn't going to happen today or maybe never. She wrung her hands and sighed.

"I'm working through some issues from my childhood. It's honestly nothing to do with the business. I love working with you, actually thrive on doing things as a team."

She took his hand and squeezed. Hers felt clammy.

"Gelsey, you have to tell me. Are you sick?"

"No, of course not. I'm perfectly fine."

"I want to know what's wrong because I care, but I'm not going to force you to open up. Just know I'm always here for you. I will do all I can to help you."

Her bottom lip quivered a bit, and he thought she might start crying, but then she set her jaw and smiled at him, the same put-on grin.

He sat back with an Eet Sum Mor in his hand, nibbling on the corners until there was a tiny crumb left which he dropped in his mouth. Gelsey stared at the TV, watching a reality dating program, something inane and rather coarse.

She glanced at him and sighed, an uneaten biscuit in her hand. "Things will be better soon. I'm sure of it." She nodded.

Then she hummed, at first quietly, almost timidly, the tune growing in clarity and volume until a melody permeated the room. Peace infused him, and her face took on a glow. Whatever happened, he knew she would be all right. Her song had once again calmed him. He'd never known a woman who both intrigued and drew out such a strong desire to protect and care for like Gelsey.

He couldn't keep his gaze off her, and this time, the smile she gave him reached her eyes.

Chapter Nine

*F*rost sprinkled the earth and the tufts of grass wherever Gelsey stepped. Her shoes crunched the glittery ice which reminded her of silver fairy dust, the dust used for a different kind of magic. When she was a fairy, her small toes would step on the ice with ease, not bothered by the cold. This morning, the cold bit into her extremities and made her nose run and eyes water.

But the frigid temperature didn't distract her. She had a destination and had never needed answers like she did today.

Walking up the steep hill on well-worn paths which soon became scarce, she came to a wooded area with a mass of wild bushes and indigenous trees. Although most of the trees were close to bare at this time of year, the wildness took her breath away, and she surveyed the town below. Newcastle spread out in a valley, varied and pretty, marred by its main industry as a backdrop to her view—Acelor Mittal Steel, spurting out its visible pollution to the air. She didn't observe for long as she needed to meet Ziana.

Tucking her head under some creepers, she followed a rocky path down a steep incline until she reached a bubbling brook running over smooth rocks. She sat down on a boulder and tapped her fingernail against it six times—Ziana's summons.

She pressed her lips together and leaned back against her hands propped on the rock. Ziana would be a small proportion of her size. When she'd said good-bye to her, she'd felt like a lumbering giant, clumsy and towering above her. It had taken some time to get used to her new height in relation to the earth and even manmade things she was vaguely familiar with in her fairy world. Her height had proven one of the least of the adjustments. The last few months had changed her perception on many things. She respected humans more—sympathized with them. She was one. In many ways, Ziana's words had been true—she had forgotten the feeling of being a fairy. But the longing for home hadn't left her. Instead it ate away at her psyche. As did the fear of hurting or being separated from Evan.

A light breeze blew the few tufts of hair sticking out of her beanie. Ziana was here. A sense of awe filled her. How odd that a fellow fairy would make goose bumps prick on her skin, lifting the hairs.

"Ziana. Don't tease me. Show yourself."

Ziana laughed and then *poof*, she turned visible on a rock just below Gelsey. Her pink wings shimmered in the dappled light. Gelsey squealed.

"I missed you so much." She stretched her hand to Ziana, and the fairy fluttered up and landed on her palm, her feet little pricks tickling her hand.

"Are you okay?" Ziana's face screwed up in concern. Although Gelsey was subordinate to Ziana, she felt almost on equal footing with her today. Was it her size, or had she grown up the last few months? Changed, matured? Did pain do such things?

"I have some serious questions. It's not a physical crisis. No one is ill. It's a mental one. I shall go crazy if I can't have answers." She took a breath, sucking in her tears. Fairies didn't cry much—not openly. Ziana would be disturbed by her outward display of distress.

"I want to know for sure that if I leave, it won't affect my husband."

"He won't remember anything."

"But his life has changed because of me. Surely, he will

84

remember something."

The fairy propped her hands on her hips. "I've told you, the gold fairy dust works like a charm. It won't let him down. And you won't remember a thing either. Neither will the people you've come into contact with. It will be as if you never met."

"But his job has changed because of me. I gave him ideas. I helped him in his business."

Ziana flitted up to a leaf on a tree and swung on it, laughing and humming as if Gelsey's concerns were nothing. She'd forgotten the frivolous fun fairies had, even older fairies. She'd become so serious over the last few weeks, especially as she'd been trying to deal with the turmoil inside of her.

For a second, she was unable to say anything, the desperate feeling inside of her like an ice capsule frozen around her. She had no way out, felt like a prisoner to her own pain. The searing pain of leaving Evan.

She had to tell Ziana. She couldn't go on else she would collapse inward.

"I can't leave him. I love him."

"You're supposed to love him." She came down and sat on the rock.

Gelsey sat next to her, surprised at how her legs trembled with the force of her feelings.

Ziana's breezy attitude irritated her but also infused a tiny drop of hope in her. If she wasn't concerned, maybe there was an answer.

"It hurts to know I'll leave him in six months and never be with him again."

"You could check on him once you're a fairy. You'd be unable to talk to him, but you probably won't even want to because you'll forget everything."

"I don't want to forget anything. Even the hard times. It's all part of love, of growing together. And if I can't remember, how can I help the queen?"

"You won't lose the memories straight away. You have to go to the palace first and talk to her. Then she will give you magic to forget."

"But Evan...will he forget straight away?"

"Not quite. But almost. You have to let go of all the memories yourself first so he will have to wait a bit, but it won't be long—maybe a day or two."

A day or two of wondering where she'd gone—of wondering if she'd left him or if she was hurt. A day or two of her wondering if she did the right thing leaving the human world.

Ziana touched her nose with her tiny hand. "Do you want to stay in the human world? You know the queen will not hold you back if you choose to stay."

Gelsey gasped. She stood up and bumped her head against the branch which became entangled in the beanie. After removing it and shaking out her hair, she spoke.

"I didn't know. Is that what happened to those other two fairies, Parye and Quea, who didn't return?"

Ziana nodded, but her expression looked serious for the first time today. "But you can never come back, then. You will lose your fairyhood forever. For eternity."

It's not like humans died and fairies didn't. Who knew what eternity held for both creatures?

Her throat tightened, and her head spun. *Never go home again?*

"I think you need to finish your commission early." Ziana zoomed around the area, her movement picking up a breeze in the sheltered spot. "I don't want Fairyland to lose you. You're a good fairy who has a great job waiting for her. The queen will despair of losing another sprite. I'm going to go back to her. I think you've learned enough about human love. All the queen wanted was for you to become embraced by it, to feel it completely so you would understand it. It seems you have. In my opinion, it's time to come home."

The fairy brushed Gelsey's cheek with her wing, and tears sprang to her eyes. *Home. Away from the pain and confusion.* She doubled over with a sharp pain in her gut. Sobs wracked through her despite her tight control since the beginning of the conversation.

"What's wrong?" Ziana buzzed around her.

"I think I'd really like that." She collapsed onto the rock, gripping her middle, afraid of the intensity of emotions. Humanity was a broken creature.

"When shall I come back here?" Gelsey said after the sobs subsided.

Ziana pulled on her hair.

"Ow."

"Wait here. You're not going anywhere."

"Okay."

"I'm going to the queen right away."

Gelsey nodded, unable to say anything, her throat clogged with so much emotion. She could leave the confusion soon and be back to her carefree yet busy life as a fairy. Her dream job waited for her—just a couple of days away. Evan would only hurt for one day. Then they would be happy again, they would be back to how they were before they met and married. Their few months together would be wiped from their consciousness forever.

The glen where she sat became dark as though the sun had gone behind a cloud. The sound of the bubbling brook seemed to mock her.

But could she do it? Could she leave the one creature who'd made her feel truly loved and needed in such a personal way? The person she enjoyed being with the most in the whole universe? Yet, her life in the human world was mundane. Putting flowers into pots and stands didn't compare to flying over mountains, rescuing animals, and watching the first buds of spring appear out of the plants.

She would never see the first spring rains falling from the sky while she hovered above—the earth changing color from dusty brown and dry to rich dark, the air weighted with moisture, and the birds flittering around in pure excitement from tree to tree. Those seasonal transitions were pure magic.

Evan's hands on her skin—touching her sensitive areas with

such skill—his love-drugged gaze upon her, sinking into her soul, the peace that came over his face after she'd brought him to climax or hummed at him until he went from frantic to calm.

Her hands in fists, she tensed every muscle in her body and screamed. There was no release for the confusion. Maybe she should go back.

Her cell phone gave a message tone. With trembling hands, she opened a voicemail from Evan.

"Hey, Gels. I can't stop thinking of you this morning. Been working hard at the factory, but your face keeps popping into my mind. I love you so much. You've changed my life forever, made it so much more meaningful. Every time I go to work, this fire burns within me because I'm making money for you, for us. It's not just a routine anymore. The whole earth looks more beautiful with you in it. The sky seems bluer, the earth even smells rich and alive, and the bird song in the morning reminds me of your soothing voice bringing peace to my soul. I will never regret the day I said, 'I do.' Those words were the best ones I'd ever spoken. Even through the hard times, we will make it. We will grow stronger and closer together. I'd better get going though. There's a client at the door."

The whole earth seemed to stand still. If it hadn't been clear to her before, right then she knew she had to stay. Yes, Evan would forget her, but he wouldn't be as happy without her. He needed her and in many ways, she needed him, too.

Standing, she tucked her phone back in her pocket and weaved her way out the glen to the open field. If she waited for Ziana, the fairy may influence her decision. No, she had to get out of there. She would never see her fairy friends again. Her new life began today.

As she came out onto a rise, the sun warmed the top of her head. She lifted her face and took in its feeble sweetness, breathing in the crisp invigorating autumn air. A skip took over her step. Maybe she hadn't lost all of her frivolous fairyness.

Goose bumps ran up her arms and neck again. A strange scent entered her being. She felt them. All over. Fairies everywhere.

Then her eyes were opened. Upon every tree, bush, and blade of grass stood sprites—some faces she recognized, others not. Why could she see them?

Ziana came right up to her and buzzed in front of her face. Gelsey almost tripped as she came to a halt.

"Where are you going?"

"I'm going back to Evan." Although she spoke with purpose, with all the fairy gazes upon her, she thought her words sounded hollow, useless, selfish, and untrue.

Yet a moment ago, she'd been so sure she was doing the right thing—following her heart.

"He needs me."

"Africa needs you, too, Gelsey," Ziana said with little emotion and no force, yet it struck a chord inside of her. "If the African Wild Cat isn't saved from extinction, it's going to cause a problem with domestic cats as they interbreed. I can't go into detail, but the queen is anxious for you to return."

Gelsey nodded. She couldn't run away. There was no choice but to return.

The fairies around her, looking at her, gave her the strength. They would help her through. She would soon not know anything of her time in the human world.

Evan would be fine without her. Yes, maybe he was happier with her in his life, but he would survive. The African Wild Cat wouldn't survive, and it seemed domestic cats would suffer, too—how she wasn't sure. It would be tragic for the whole human race. She'd seen how humans depended on their cats for much comfort—Evan's mother was one of those people.

"I'll come." She wiped a tear from the corner of her eye and stared at the town of Newcastle below. Part of her wished that in another universe she could flit from one world to another—be a fairy during the day, but then at night and on weekends, be a wife to Evan.

"You look unhappy." Ziana flew around her head, almost restless. The other fairies flew from branch to branch, as if unsure of her commitment.

She sank onto the ground. They waited for her. Her heart called out to Evan—she wanted to send a message back to him to say how much he'd changed her. How he had taught her the depths of soul that came from loving someone. Love made her unselfish and gave her peace, how it filled a spot in her she'd never known was empty. Evan had evoked that from her. Sure, the fairy dust had started the magic, but he'd sprinkled his love magic on her. Would the love magic depart forever? Her gift in calming the distressed had never left her when she entered the human world. Some things remained.

Ziana settled on a tuft of grass before her. Her fairy's wings fluttered gently, her face was so at peace, so sweet. How she missed being like her.

"If I stay...." She focused on Ziana. If she saw the expressions of the other fairies, she would feel the guilt again of letting down her own species. "Will I be able to see you? Maybe I can help the African Wild Cat as a human."

Ziana sighed, her wings touching with annoyance. "Gelsey, you have to know something. Your human loves you. But if he finds out the truth, will he still love you?"

She shrugged.

"If you stay, you will have to tell him, else the magic will turn bad."

What did she mean?

"Because you're not going to sprinkle the gold dust on him a second time, the magic will start to turn bad. It's only designed to last a year."

"Bad in what way?"

"His love will turn wrong. He will want you all to himself and no one else can touch you. You will become like a slave to him."

Gelsey clutched her knees together and squeezed them. She shook her head, tears coming to her eyes again. "No, he wouldn't do such a thing. I know he's not like that."

Ziana's wings became frantic. "I'm not lying to you. You have to believe me. The queen told me this a moment ago. You have to tell him who you are and why you came to the earth. Once you do tell him, the gold dust will have no hold on him or you. You may continue in your human world without any influence from the fairy world. You can stay in your new life unharmed."

"I can't tell him." She shook her head, tears flooding her vision. She saw nothing ahead of her, no fairies, no town, no grass or trees...just pain. If Evan knew, he wouldn't trust the love between them any longer. If the magic was broken, would they still want each other? Could she risk staying in the human world forever and still lose her reason for being there?

Ziana's wings quieted. All of a sudden, Gelsey understood. The fairies were here to support her, to help her through this very painful decision. They loved her as much as Evan did. Fairies didn't appear to humans, but today, she'd been gifted with a whole crowd of them before her eyes. They'd risked discovery and therefore death by appearing to her because, by becoming visible to her, they would be visible to any other human who came by.

And what guarantee did she have Evan would love her forever? She'd seen Marissa's bitter divorce—her love story had gone bad. Just by coming into contact with people every day, by watching the TV screen by night, and by reading, she'd seen how many broken relationships and marriages there were in the human world. Love was wracked with uncertainty and pain. Instead, her fairy home was a solid, reliable world, filled with its own magic—one she could depend on.

She stood up and brushed dry grass off her jeans.

"I'm coming home." Tears filled her eyes once again, but they were tears of relief and joy.

The fairies broke out in a song mixed with the hum of their wings.

"Come quick," Ziana touched her hand. "Come to the glen." There was a consummate hum of activity as everyone converged to the spot where she'd summoned Ziana earlier.

"Stand there." The fairy pointed to the boulder. "Close your eyes."

She screwed her wet eyes shut and waited. The feeling of fairy dust on her head then shoulders and lastly toes sent pure bliss through her—every part of her body tingled and joy entered her being.

"You can open your eyes." Ziana's voice sounded deeper and louder.

She popped them open to find a large Ziana before her. She pressed the muscles on her back together. Her wings whooshed and lifted her a bit. The boulder appeared huge to her.

"I'm home." She laughed and flew around, ecstatic to have her wings back. Unable to resist, she stretched around and caressed the silky-soft wing on her right with her hand.

Ziana laughed with her and took her left hand. "Let's get you to the queen before you change your mind."

"No, I won't. I'm sure of this." Several of the other fairies still hovered around, and they followed them to the palace.

"Pinny will fly to Evan and sprinkle some gold dust on him so you don't have to do it," Ziana assured her. "That way, he won't remember anything and you're not tempted to stay with him."

Gelsey nodded, pushing all thoughts of Evan out of her mind.

On the way to the palace, Gelsey understood why Ziana didn't let go of her hand, because she began to doubt she could ever forget Evan. Doubt she'd done the right thing.

Chapter Ten

As soon as he came home, Evan knew. He walked from room to room, looking for her, but knew she'd gone.

He sank onto the bed and wrapped his head in his arms, unable to even look at the ceiling, which reminded him of those many nights they'd chatted until midnight on their bed, staring at the boards. He could tell her the most inane stories of his childhood, and she would listen, entranced. On occasion, she'd taken his hand and squeezed it as if her life depended on it.

The whole day, the restlessness stayed with him. She hadn't replied to his message in the morning. When he phoned the florist, Marissa had said Gelsey hadn't come in yet, which was unusual. His wife was devoted to her job.

Had she been abducted?

He called her phone, but it just rang and then went to voicemail. He called the network provider to find out if they could trace any calls made by her number, but there were none.

Was there someone else?

Did she have another life?

The doubts he'd pushed away when he packed up her home assaulted him again. There were lots of unanswered questions about her life. He'd never met any of her family, which wasn't strange seeing they'd been married only a few months. But even a phone call or a Skype session? Nothing. The stories of her childhood were broken and rather incomplete. He'd put it down to being an only child and having a rather lonely childhood. Many people with difficult pasts blocked out part of them so as not to face up to the pain.

Could she be running from something? Had she taken on another identity for some reason?

Although Gelsey had always been pure and wonderful to him, maybe she'd lied. He struggled to believe it the more he thought about it. The times they'd shared had seemed so genuine.

Why had she left? Her pain the day before had been real. Because she'd known she would leave soon and felt deep sorrow?

"Ugh...." He squeezed his forehead. The questions didn't stop, the throbbing ache in his gut worsened until he felt sick inside.

Jumping up, he rummaged through her stuff, trying to find a clue somewhere—an indication of another life, another address, a mission, something. But he found nothing. She had many more belongings since their marriage. That warmed his heart. It had been a pleasure working his butt off providing for her. Money was no longer an issue to him. Yes, his savings account was lower than before, but his heart had been full every time he'd bought her a new dress or a stylish pair of shoes.

Exhausted, he neatened up her belongings. His cell phone rang in his pocket. He answered with hope but then heard Marissa's voice.

"Evan, have you found her yet?"

"No."

"Have you gone to the police?"

"It's too soon."

"I wish you'd told me something was wrong."

"I didn't think it was this serious. Please. Do you know anything about her life before you hired her at the florist? You should have her curriculum vitae and details."

"Come to the shop. I'm not that busy. I haven't been able to concentrate anyway."

"I'm on my way."

He left the mess and locked up. Within twenty minutes, he stood opposite Marissa in the cramped florist shop.

Her eyes were red and a little puffy. Evan, for once the whole day, thought of someone other than Gelsey.

"I've been giving her so much work lately. Maybe I overloaded her and she couldn't take it." Marissa fiddled with an arrangement, putting grasses and greenery in and then taking them out again, not following a specific strategy. She seemed oblivious to her crazy behavior.

"I think it went deeper than that." Evan felt a sudden calm. He would find her, no matter what it took. "She seemed troubled yesterday."

"What about? I've noticed her moods haven't been great. Have you been fighting?" Marissa gave him a penetrating stare as if this whole thing was his fault.

"Not at all. Everything was good between us. Too good." His whole body went weary and weak. He slumped, setting his elbows on the counter and resting his head into his hands.

Was it all a crazy, happy dream? Some days, he had fought thoughts that their love was too good to be true, that one day she would be snatched away from him. Like Trisha.

His previous determination faded into a choking inertia. If he couldn't stop Trisha from dying and leaving him, how could he stop Gelsey from disappearing from his life? He'd somehow known since then he was destined to be a loner.

"I'm sorry." Marissa threw down the arrangement with a clunk. "We can't just stand here and talk about it. Let's do something."

"I know."

He helped Marissa clean up and lock the shop even though it was only two in the afternoon.

"Where do we start?" he asked when she climbed in next to him in the cab of his truck.

"I have no idea."

ભ

The opulence of the palace eased some of Gelsey's fears. She flew in with more confidence this time, aware of the sense of growth she'd experienced the last few months. The heated air of the palace also took away the involuntary shaking that had overcome her since Ziana had brought her back to her home. Fairies looked at her with warmth and kindness, thawing out her heart even further.

Her wings ached, though. She hadn't used them for a while, and they'd flown quite a distance. The tension hadn't helped her with flying. She had begged Ziana to stop several times much to the energetic fairy's dismay. Several nights out in the cold, huddled inside the hollow of a tree or in a cave had magnified the pain of saying good-bye to Evan. If Ziana hadn't held her constantly with a strong sense of duty, she'd have given up days ago. The other fairies had dispersed to their respective areas along the way, but Ziana held on fast. Her assurances that it was for the best for both Evan and her had kept her going.

Meeting other fairies along the way had spurred her on. All the savannah fairies knew her name—word had spread of how she'd been successful in completing her commission—a crazy thing to say since she hadn't met with the queen yet. They were confident in her beyond her capabilities. They held a new respect in their eyes.

Being unable to eat much during the whole journey had drained her of the little strength she'd possessed. Ziana seemed to sense she couldn't move fast through the palace. She called for a male servant to help her. They took Gelsey by the hands and flew with her the last stretch to the queen's conference room.

The queen wasn't there, so Gelsey sat on a plush velvet seat as instructed by one of the posh attendants. She rested her head against the back and sighed. What if the queen came in and saw her like this? What questions would she ask her? Would she pass her commission? Would the magic really erase all memories of Evan? Would she forever wonder if she'd abandoned him? Had she done the right thing? She didn't know if she could take anymore strain. Exhaustion and grief took over, making her whole body want to sag into the sofa. Where was the frivolous fun feeling of being a fairy? Maybe the dregs of humanity still lurked in her. Just as it had taken time to forget what it felt like to be a fairy, so she would probably need time to adapt to her home again.

An attendant fluttered toward her, her wings glowing blue and green, her matching outfit a-glitter with light. They were magnificent—the palace fairies. How did they feel being trapped inside most of the day, though? For an earth fairy, it would be torture. But the attendant seemed happy and carried herself with an air of self-respect and quiet satisfaction.

"The queen wishes for you to come into her living room. She has a surprise." The fairy smiled, her soft, pearly skin wrinkled with the force of it.

Gelsey gave a weak grin back and followed her out, every limb of her body and vein of her wings achy and stiff.

The journey to the living room took her through many passages and chambers. At times, she thought she would faint. Ziana had disappeared, and the palace fairy didn't even look back to check on her but seemed to assume she would be fine keeping up with her speed. Every ounce of her small reserves of energy pulled her forward. She only had to get through a few hours and then all the pain would be over. Her dream lay just around the corner. The idea somehow didn't excite her as much as she would have hoped. Instead, it continued to bloom a sense of unease inside her she'd never experienced before. A deep knowing she would regret her decision to leave Evan for the rest of her life.

Perhaps she was too tired and drained from the difficult decisions. Hunger robbed her of logic.

Every passage led to beautiful rooms, shining with jewels and decorated with naturals like dried mushrooms, grasses, and flowers and sculpted stones and wooden structures. Fairy art graced most walls, unique in its lack of order and ability to emulate nature, toning down the gaudiness of the jeweled light fittings, doorknobs, and ornaments. She remembered the simple décor of her and Evan's bedroom and longed to collapse upon the bed, take his hand, and chat about her day.

"You may go in the room. I can't come. Only special guests are allowed in the queen's living room," the fairy spoke, her voice softer, almost timid.

Gelsey nodded, unsure why the queen had chosen her, having almost decided to abandon the fairies. If she knew the doubts pulling her away, screaming inside her to fly away back to the grove above Newcastle, back to her home, she wouldn't have invited her into her personal space.

The attendant flew off, and Gelsey remained alone, unable to move while darkness overtook her.

The door opened, and there stood the queen. She struggled to focus on her face, everything around her a haze. The queen clasped her and picked her up with her large arms. Gelsey felt lighter than air. Then she remembered nothing else.

Chapter Eleven

The police, Marissa, Evan's friends, and people who had met Gelsey in her few short months in Newcastle, joined the pair to scour the area for her. After Evan and Marissa had been driving around for an hour, Marissa phoned a police friend who'd told her there was no waiting period to file a missing person's report in South Africa. If a family or friend suspected someone missing, that was enough.

They went straight to the police station.

The next few days were frantic. Evan slept little. He gave the officers some of her belongings, and they even used their sniffer dogs to try to trace her.

All bus and taxi services were questioned as to the possibility of her going out of town. Nothing. Gelsey didn't own a car, so she couldn't have gone far. Word went out to neighboring towns to look out for her, as well as to the Durban and Johannesburg airports.

"We are going to start searching the uninhabited areas as she might have gone for a walk," said Officer Dlamini to Evan who sat in his car with the engine running, trying to think where else to look.

"I thought you'd done that already."

"Not everywhere."

Hope surged through him again. Despite the exhaustion, he shifted the truck into reverse. "I'm going to Signal Hill."

"We'll meet you there." The officer straightened and ran to his car. He'd been Evan's pillar the last few days.

He drove up the steep hill leading to the pinnacle of the town. His heart raced. What if she'd fallen down somewhere or been attacked in the bush? Gelsey loved the outdoors. She'd withdrawn from her habitual walks in the garden since she'd been depressed, but maybe she'd decided a good stroll would bring some joy back into her life, unaware of the dangers to a woman out alone in secluded places in South Africa.

Why hadn't he thought of this before?

His cell phone rang. He pulled to the side of the road. *Marissa.* "Hi."

"There's something strange going on," she told him.

"What do you mean?"

"You remember when you first met Gelsey?"

"How could I forget?" His breath sucked out of him, and his chest ached. She'd stolen his heart almost straight away. Would he ever see her again?

"Remember the gold glitter she sprinkled over you and the arrangement you were buying from us?"

"Yes, it was beautiful just like her." He recalled he'd found some of the stuff on the bed a couple of mornings ago. It had gotten all over his hair. Gelsey must have done some crafts on the bed and forgotten to clean it up.

"I kept some of it. She didn't know, but a few sprinkles landed behind a container on the floor behind the counter. I put it in a small box and kept it in my cupboard. It was so beautiful and so unlike anything I'd seen before. You can't really feel it if you picked it up and...."

"Marissa, I have to go. I doubt this is as important as the search. It's going to be dark in four hours, and I think I know where she may have gone."

"Wait, Evan. This might be important. That gold stuff...it's magic. I had it in a box. Whenever I touched it, I got a new customer at the shop or something wonderful happened to my daughter at school."

"I can't see the relevance to Gelsey."

"This glitter was Gelsey's. She had a whole lot of it. Don't you remember her sprinkling it on your flower arrangement when you first came into the florist?"

"Yes, yes, whatever. Listen, this 'magic' you're talking about is all coincidence. Probably in your mind." He sighed. "I know it's your contact with her, your memory of her, but it's not going to help us find Gelsey."

"The gold is magic. I know it."

The trauma of the last few days had gotten to Marissa. The woman was falling to pieces. "We're going to find her. Don't give up yet."

"I'm not giving up. I think this is the clue. I think Gelsey is magic."

"There's no such a thing as magic. This is the real world here. We need to find her." He put the phone down before he could hear anymore. Marissa was right, Gelsey had sprinkled gold dust all over him. What had prompted her to do such a strange thing?

He pushed Marissa's crazy words and all the questions away from his mind. He couldn't worry about the older woman and her strange theories. Finding Gelsey would solve all the problems and bring Marissa down to earth again.

ᦉ

A soft wetness rested on her forehead. Gelsey's eyes popped open. The queen's face poised close to hers. She jerked up and away, and then wooziness took over.

"Just relax. You fainted. I honestly cannot believe any of my attendants didn't notice how dehydrated and exhausted you are."

As her eyes refocused, she saw what the queen had placed on her—a moss cloth—the surefire way to revive an exhausted fairy. The musty-moss smell permeated her nostrils, reviving her some. The queen pressed it against her, and Gelsey smiled.

"Thanks."

"Now, please, drink some dew tea."

She took several sips, the sweetness almost burning her tongue with its intense flavor. Each sip seeped more strength into her.

On a table next to the chaise she perched on lay a spread that made her stomach contract. "Oh, the food looks wonderful."

"Tuck in."

"But...."

"I'm not going to talk to you until you have more strength. I know you are anxious to have the gold dust sprinkled on you to take the memories away. I won't wait too long but you need to eat first. And I'm not going anywhere. You shall not be alone anymore until your full fairyhood has been restored." The queen's gentle words and the warm kindness in her gaze gave Gelsey the strength she needed to eat.

Her stomach had shrunk. She couldn't take in much but, after several delicious bites, her strength revived enough so her wings could flutter again. Running her hands over her precious limbs, she relished their velvety rippling power, each bump a glorious part of their muscular strength. She'd missed them so much.

The queen obviously understood her pleasure and sat opposite her, an amused smile on her face.

"Good to be winged again?"

"Wonderful."

"I'm so proud of you for choosing to put the earth first."

Gelsey nodded. Yes, she'd done well but had she sacrificed her heart forever?

"You won't regret it. In a few hours."

Gelsey nodded because the queen would wish her to agree, but everything in her screamed against it—except for the pull of her wings as they grew stronger with each bite of nourishment. She pushed the food away, fighting twinges of nausea.

"Please may we start?" She hated having to plead with the

queen but couldn't bear to wait any longer.

"I think you are ready. The fire has come back into your eyes. Now, Gelsey, why are the humans pulling away from having children?"

"They aren't all pulling away."

"We are aware the population appears to be growing well still, but the humans who care more for the balance of the planet are the ones who seem less eager to have babies."

"I suppose those who are educated use ways to control how many children they have. It's difficult to be human. There is much pain and life is hard."

"They have made it hard for themselves with their foolishness."

Before, she would have agreed with the queen, but having lived as a human made her want to defend them. Evan wasn't foolish. He was wise and loving and wonderful.

"I see you have experienced love with this human man just as we intended. It seems to have grown faster than we thought. Human love is a hard thing for fairies to understand. It seems to be very emotional and not useful except to make children."

"'Tis not true. Love holds families together. It keeps couples bonded so they may look after their kids."

The queen nodded as if she pondered her statement. "Is their emotional love strong enough to last?"

"Possibly the problem. I don't think it lasts so much anymore. Well, there are many people who are hurt and disillusioned by love. Maybe the reason why they don't have children so much anymore is because they don't stick to one partner like they used to."

"How can we help them change?"

Gelsey stared at the queen. The monarch assumed she knew everything. She felt powerless to answer the question. Would she fail her commission?

"I don't know. I haven't stayed with my human male long enough to know the answer. There are couples who do make it last until they die, but I don't know the secret. It seems very few do."

"The fickle human love. Why can't they reproduce for the sake of the race, not for the sake of their feelings?"

"I think their love is often unselfish and caring. It's not fickle."

"Are you sure that is not what the hormones want you to think? The female hormones to draw you to the man."

Gelsey sighed. Evan would lay down his life for her—well, so she'd thought. The queen made her doubt it. She did doubt he could love her enough when he found out the truth, partly why she'd left.

"Do you not think the love a human has for their child is strong?" Gelsey asked, remembering how upset Marissa had been one day when her daughter had been bullied at school. She'd marched into the school and stood up for her child against the principal even though they'd assured her the daughter overreacted. Marissa had eventually taken Delia out of the school and put her in another one. And it had been a more expensive one. Her friend was a single mother who laid down her life for her child.

"I know it is strong. They don't seem to have failed in that regard...well, the majority of them."

"Maybe if more of the human men were like my man, the world would be stronger."

The queen shook her head. "He wasn't anything special. He merely had the magic upon him."

Gelsey shook her head and then stopped at the look the queen gave her. She knew what she thought—as soon as Gelsey had forgotten him, she wouldn't think these human thoughts anymore.

Was she so deceived?

"But what if we sprinkled magic on all the men so they would love their women?" Gelsey somehow doubted the gold dust had made Evan who he was. Something about him made her believe in him despite everything. He loved her like no other creature ever had. How could she survive without him? She pictured his face, filled with anguish, and she had no means to sing to him and calm him. Was he in pain since her disappearance?

The queen touched her arm. "Please, Gelsey. We haven't much further to go. Don't draw back."

"Why did you send me there? I haven't helped at all." Her voice came out whiny.

"You have helped more than we expected. In your eyes, I see the power of human love. I see it has its own magic. We shouldn't work against it. We should work with it. The more love there is, the more children will come."

"Are you sure? I thought you called it a fickle emotion."

She smiled. "It is, but it makes families happen."

"How can we help human love, then?"

"Fairies have ways."

Gelsey smiled for the first time in a long time. "What a good job that would be."

"You might not like it so much once your memory of love has been wiped. You will think the humans stupid."

She clamped her lips shut and suppressed a sigh.

"Are you ready?"

She held silent and still, unable to nod in agreement. Instead, she hummed to soothe herself, but this time it did no such thing. So, she pictured Evan closing his eyes and lying back on the bed, at peace from her calming song. Her hand was in his, the warmth from his closeness entered her being.

"Gelsey." The queen shook her. "Think of your time last spring when you helped the butterflies in Namibia by moving them to the grasslands. They wouldn't have survived the heat wave if you hadn't completed your commission."

She nodded, the memories clear. At first, the butterflies had been annoying—erratic and slow, often stopping to chat along the way. Those colorful yellow butterflies were more frivolous than any fairy, especially to accompany across country. A smile came to her, calming her lethal thoughts. She'd almost given up on her commission to save the African Wild Cat because of fickle human love. She'd helped one once. It looked so much like a domestic cat, yet it had an earthiness no domestic cat could hold—an inner strength and power, a connection with the planet.

"I believe you're the only one who can save the African Wild Cat."

How did the queen know her thoughts?

"I trust you will endure through the difficult task. You've borne so much the last few months."

Tears came to her eyes, and she sank her arms into her abdomen, the pain of the confusion she'd suffered brought to the fore by the queen's understanding. The monarch rose and walked to a glass shelf displaying shimmering golden vases in an array of shapes and designs. *The vessels for the gold dust. Sacred and precious in fairyland.* Gold dust couldn't be wasted. A select few used it, and the substance was sprinkled on fairies and humans who needed it the most. Longing for the confusion to end turned to hope.

Her gaze fixed on two silver urns on the very top shelf. They probably contained silver dust. Ordinary fairies like her didn't know the purpose of silver dust. Rare as it was, very few fairies touched it. She turned away. Why would she need to know unless the magic was entrusted to her?

She didn't have the energy for anything to be entrusted to her. She just wanted to lie on her bed at home and listen to music or chat with Evan beside her as he worked on a crossword puzzle. Oh, to relax and do nothing and be responsible for nothing but making flowers look nice. How could she handle being responsible for a whole species?

The queen approached her with a gold jar shaped like a bell. She dipped her fingers into the vase and pulled out a small pouch that shimmered in the soft lamplight of her intimate room. With steady, skilled fingers, she opened the little purse.

Gelsey closed her eyes, waiting for the dust to fall on her. Everything converged on her in one moment. All her dreams seemed to come together into a hard, dark mass that lodged in her throat and put cruel fingers around her heart. She would never be with him again, never share the oneness, the passion. She wanted to die because she'd just lost the most important thing in her life. Was it possible for a fairy to suffer so much?

გ

The sun had gone down an hour before, and the night air cut into Evan's throat. He glanced at the sky, disoriented. Why was he on the top of Signal Hill in the middle of nowhere with a flashlight in his hand?

A police car bleeped and drove off in the distance.

After the dizziness passed, he found a path with the beam and walked to the closest road. His car was parked there with the door unlocked and the window down—a crazy thing to do on a deserted road in South Africa. What had he been thinking?

For the life of him, he couldn't remember what he'd been looking for. Should he get his head examined?

A desperate hunger pang jarred him from his confusing thoughts. When last had he eaten? A pounding headache alerted him to the fact he'd been sleep deprived for days. Besides that, he felt fine and upbeat. His business was starting to take off since he'd just set up equipment to make his own solar panels. Without having to pay the middle man, his profit margins would be much higher. Things were looking up.

The upbeat feeling didn't last as he started up his engine— the crazy sinking feeling in his gut likely resulted from a lack of sleep and explained why he was doing inexplicable things. Maybe he'd been working too hard, staying late into the night sometimes to get things running. He should catch up on some sleep and food since his business was taking off again.

He climbed into his car, surprised by how achy his muscles felt, and drove into town to find some food.

Thankfully, it wasn't too late and the KFC was open. He went through the drive-through and ordered a large meal and an ice cream cone to keep him going while he drove home.

Home felt much warmer than outside. He emptied the

contents of the brown bag onto a plate, came into the lounge and switched on the TV. He couldn't help gobbling down the food. He should balance out home and work more. It didn't pay to get his body into such a state where he couldn't even work or think properly.

He stared at the TV not really seeing it, then glanced around the lounge. Something was missing. The house seemed empty. Had he sold some stuff to pay for equipment? No, the emptiness went deeper. He tried to shake an awful uneasy feeling. Was he remembering Trisha tonight?

He did tend to think of her when tired and vulnerable.

The bond between twins was intense. Trisha had been his best friend. Losing her had taken a piece of his heart away. He'd survived, yes. But the emptiness from her death seemed to haunt him more than ever. Why did he feel so damn empty inside when things were going so well?

Chapter Twelve

"*I*'m thrilled to have you back again." Bitty bumped Gelsey's wing with her green one and made her lose her footing on a branch of a pine tree on a farm in Zululand. The area had been her home before her commission. Bitty giggled and flew to a higher branch on another tree.

"Hey, I hate it when you do that." She had a smile on her face, though. The pleasure at seeing her friend had been joy compounded upon joy. She'd come out of a dark tunnel into the light. Good thing she couldn't remember the pain but knew she'd experienced it to the "nth" degree. Like the feeling she had after recovering from a horrible fairy flu and started getting her energy back—the feeling of coming alive again and gratefulness she'd made it through.

"The gold dust worked its magic as usual." Bitty flew to the top of a hedge outside a human farmhouse and sat on a group of pine needles.

Gelsey fingered some of the fleshy tubes while the fresh minty fragrance surrounded her. Pine trees were wonderful. They didn't lose their invigorating smell in fall. In the coastal Zululand, many tropical plants kept their greenery throughout winter.

"I heard how miserable you were."

"You did? I don't remember, but the fairies along my journey from the palace told me how scared they were for me and how brave I was. Word has spread all over fairyland."

"You were very brave." Bitty dove down and knocked her playfully with her foot on the wing. Gelsey tumbled over and did a flip in the air. She righted herself and propped her hands on her hips. She'd forgotten how Bitty could dive and knock her off balance.

"I'll get you." She soared toward her friend and pulled her wings.

"Ouch."

"Aw, come on. That wasn't sore."

"I'll have to buy wing guards now that you're back again."

"Not for long." Gelsey settled on some needles again, more serious. "What are you doing?"

"I'm in between jobs. I'm going to work with weeds." She pulled a face. Bitty was a plant fairy and super talented.

"What? They want weeds to flourish?"

"Sometimes it's necessary."

"Hard to believe.

"We always have to follow instructions, even if they don't make sense."

Gelsey nodded. She knew that much. Her body seemed to jar, and she sucked in a few shaky breaths. She clung onto a pine needle to steady herself. Was she coming down with something?

"You look nervous. Are you ready for your new job?"

"I'm totally ready. Been ready for years."

"You're going to cinch it." Bitty came and stood next to her, and they watched some dragonflies flitter around.

"Winter's coming in a few weeks. I'm not ready for it."

"No one ever is." Bitty sat down and sighed. "I wish I could come with you."

"Me, too." Suddenly, Gelsey couldn't bear to go it alone. She took her friend's hand and squeezed it hard.

Bitty stared at her, her eyes wide. "You okay?"

She shrugged. There shouldn't be anything wrong. She was excited for her job. Maybe she'd missed Bitty more than she realized.

The fairy with leaf-green wings pulled away and shot toward the top of a tall palm tree. Ever moving. Why did fairies never sit still?

She was one. What was she thinking?

They spent a few more hours together, picking flowers and making arrangements.

"Where did you learn to do it?" Bitty asked her as Gelsey made an array of bunches and set them in a circle on a field.

"All fairies know how to make art with nature. It's in our blood."

Bitty shook her head. "You've always been in tune with the insects and animals, not so much plants."

"I have. I love plants." She flapped her wings together, relishing the feel of them rubbing against one another. Her wings felt strong. Her body was primed and ready for her new job. The few weeks of rest at the palace after her commission in the human world had done her a world of good.

Bitty rolled her eyes.

She would allow her friend to remain the master of plants in her own mind. "It was just an artistic whim. I don't know where it came from. Maybe it's my way of preparing for my new job."

But where had she learned how to arrange flowers so well? Had she carried through a talent from her time in the human world? She couldn't remember anything from then. All she remembered was she'd succeeded in her commission and the queen's delight with her. All she needed to know.

Excitement threaded through her, making her wings buzz at fever pitch. She was all ready to go.

"Bitty, I'm going to start flying out now." She patted her friend on the shoulder. "I can't wait any longer."

She smiled. "Okay." She peered at the sky through some tree branches. "It's going to get dark soon."

"I can get two hours of flying done before the sun sets. It will take me about two days to get there. The place where the cats live is in the north eastern part of South Africa. Some humans have a conservation center to help them, but they're not doing enough. They are still dying out."

"Good luck." Bitty gave her a wing tap and flitted away.

Gelsey shook her head. Had her friend always been so shallow? She seemed to care to a degree, but good-byes were ordinary, not charged with emotion. It may be some time before she saw her fairy friend again.

She flicked her wings to give her some height above the trees and set on her journey. Good thing she had a solid sense of direction. Bitty cared but was distracted by her obsession with plants. Had she been like that, too? Maybe her commission had matured her quite a bit. She hoped to find a fairy friend where she would be working with whom she could identify. As exciting as this job was, she wondered if it would be lonely—not a common emotion for her. In fact, she wondered how many fairies ever felt lonesome. There was always a crowd of fairies around, always someone to talk to. Right that minute, several fairies flew past her while others sat on trees or worked on the ground below. Yet, she felt distanced from them, of another plane. Was it because she was on a higher level to them? Were they withdrawing from her because she had completed a difficult commission?

She flicked her wings harder and pushed herself. Maybe nerves gripped her for her new job and played with her mind. She concentrated on the journey and watched the sun set, splashing warm color across the sky. The air grew icy as soon as the sun started setting. Gelsey flew down into a wooded area and found a tree stump with a good-sized hole in it. She settled in for the night, wrapping her wings around herself to keep warm.

Strange dreams troubled her. She woke up several times, staring at a small sliver of moon visible through the hole in the stump and the branches of trees. She'd dreamed of holding a male fairy's hand and talking while lying on a soft mat. The fairy laughed and stared at her in a fascinating way as though he saw deep into her, as if he knew all the doubts and fears she fought. Then she dreamed of soaring on the wind with this fairy, dancing in the sky with him.

Sleep eluded her. She stared at the moon and hummed. A haunting and hollow song came out. Whatever was the matter with her? She'd never felt this unease before. She couldn't tell anyone about it. They might withdraw her from her new job, thinking she hadn't recovered from her human commission.

In time, she fell asleep with a song on her mind she'd never heard before.

C&#x8;

Evan marched into the little florist shop in the town arcade and approached the counter. If he didn't get Sandy a bunch of flowers today, he would lose the courage and never do it.

"I'd like a bunch of flowers. Not roses, something different," he said to the middle-aged brunette at the counter.

"*Déjà vu*," she said, gazing at him with a peculiar expression on her face.

"I'm sorry?"

"What happened just seemed really familiar, as though I'd experienced it before."

He shrugged. "What do you have?" If she would just hurry before he changed his mind. He was attracted to Sandy but didn't feel anything for her. He wondered if he could ever feel anything for a woman. Had his twin sister's sudden death as a ten-year-old done that to him?

No, he had to push those thoughts away and give her a chance. Sandy was pretty with her straight blonde bob, delicate smooth skin, and soft blue eyes. Her tenderness toward horses showed she would be a kind person. He would be crazy not to go for her. She always seemed excited to see him when he came to finish installations at the lodges. This was his second installation on the same property this year as the lodge had built several more cottages that needed solar panel geysers. Sandy ran the stables and took the tourists on horse rides in the area.

"Come around behind the counter and pick some flowers out

of these buckets."

"Okay." He obeyed, staring down at the metal buckets and containers with flowers, grasses, and leafy plants. A strange sensation jerked through him, robbing him of breath. He fumbled for something to grasp onto to steady himself.

"Are you okay?" the shop lady asked.

"*Déjà vu.*" He laughed.

She laughed, too, but then stared at him, a frown on her face. "Have you come in here before?"

"No. I've been meaning to get a bunch of flowers for weeks but never had the courage."

"Is it for a lady?"

He nodded.

"Want something special for it? It's free."

"What?" He picked some flowers, handing her the bunch, and went back to his spot around the counter.

"I found this little container in my house." She opened a tiny box which held some very fine gold glitter, probably used for crafts. Odd how much it looked almost like powder and how it shimmered in the shop's dim lighting. "Touch it."

He tentatively put his hand inside but felt nothing against his skin except a strange tingling sensation go up his arm.

A series of pictures of a beautiful woman's face flashed through his mind. He pulled back, reeling, and almost stumbled over a vase on the floor.

"Are you okay?"

"Yes. The glitter feels odd. I think I'll pass on putting it on the flowers.

The pictures had been so vivid. He knew the woman from somewhere. She was the most beautiful lady he'd seen, with her long curly hair in a rich chestnut color. Who was she?

"I'd like to pay."

The florist lady still fiddled with the gold dust as though she found it sacred. She sprinkled it on her arm and smiled, a dreamy look on her face.

"I wouldn't touch that if I were you." *Whoa.* Did he just blurt that out?

"Why?" She glanced at him, and he felt a strange kinship with the woman almost as if she were a mother or sister. First, the unexplained occurrence up on Signal Hill with him standing there holding a flashlight in the dark, then the horrible empty feeling hounding him wherever he went, and now this.

"Do we know each other?" he asked.

"I wondered the same thing. I don't recognize your face, but there's something." She shook her head. "This week is getting stranger and stranger. First, my daughter found me slumped on my bed in the afternoon. I'd slept for hours without eating or sleeping. She said she didn't know what was wrong with me. Then, I found this funny box in my cupboard by my jewelry. I don't remember putting it there. I can't stop looking at it and touching the stuff inside of it."

"It's creepy. I got a strange feeling when I touched it."

"I feel happy when I touch it, like all my problems seem to fade away."

"I've always been a logical person." He shook his head. "I think I've been working too hard and, with lack of sleep and food, I've been seeing and doing strange things."

She smiled and nodded. "Maybe we both need a holiday."

The woman was right. He thought too much into this whole thing. She handed him his debit card and a slip, having completed the transaction without him noticing.

"Oh, thanks. What's your name?"

"It's Marissa."

"I'm Evan. Hopefully, I'll be back sometime. It'll mean the flowers were a success."

Marissa nodded but looked down, once again transfixed by the little box and its contents. He grabbed his bouquet of flowers and walked out the shop.

Once he took the road toward Sandy, he relaxed. It was all a product of too much work and not enough relaxation. Problem was he couldn't take leave as it was his own business, and he didn't have anyone to stand in for him.

Twenty minutes later, he stood out on the field, waiting for Sandy to come back from a quick ride on her horse. He held the bunch of flowers, feeling more and more uncomfortable about it. As soon as she came near him, she would know. He couldn't run away. Yet, he had to make a move. Casual dating wasn't doing it for him anymore. The need to settle down with someone for life had become overwhelming. He'd never been the settling type. Poor Sandy. Was she ready for this?

Chapter Thirteen

*A*lthough Gelsey didn't remember where she'd done her commission in the human world, she had a sense she flew over the place at present. She'd been flying for hours since the sun had risen, and a magnetic force seemed to pull her toward the ground. She fought it. She had good height, just below the clouds. The air currents were perfect for speed. If she kept going, she would make good distance today and get to her new place of work early tomorrow. How she longed to meet her first African Wild Cat. Well, the animals seldom ever saw the fairies—it would upset them—but she couldn't wait to touch the cat, feel its fur beneath her fingers.

Yet, something pulled her downward. Something strong, an inner compulsion she'd never felt before—a deep hunger and force.

She had to investigate this feeling. It would distract her from her job, so she needed to deal with it once and for all. The queen had promised she would forget everything from the human world. She'd forgotten everything in her mind, but her heart hadn't. Maybe the gold dust magic wasn't strong enough to wipe everything.

Before she could change her mind, she dove down onto a field below. A woman on a horse galloped through the field, the wind blowing her blonde hair peeking out from under her helmet like liquid sunlight. She was a beautiful human, and she worked in harmony with the horse. Gelsey followed her, flying inches above her head.

She slowed as she came to several buildings. A man stood on the field, flowers in his hand. He waited for her. Ah, the human love. The very reason for her commission.

She kept above the lady's head as she came to the man with dark hair and even darker, piercing eyes.

Her heart raced like crazy. Huh? The last few minutes she had been flying slower, slower than she had the whole morning, yet she felt out of breath.

Her gaze fixed on him. He wasn't particularly handsome from a fairy point of view, but his eyes held her in a trance. He looked right at her, not at the woman on the horse.

"Hi," the blonde said. "How are you, Evan?" She climbed off the horse, removed her helmet, and came to him.

He said nothing, but just stared at Gelsey. Humans almost never saw fairies. Only on very rare occasions when a human transcended the realms. Was this one of those times?

"What's wrong?" the woman asked.

"I don't know. I keep seeing strange things." He looked away and rubbed his forehead, ruffling his bangs until they stuck up at sharp angles.

She liked this human very much. She didn't want to leave him.

"What are the flowers for?"

"Um, I thought you would like them." He handed them to her with a clumsy movement but kept on glancing at Gelsey. She considered flying away, but her wings refused to accelerate but just fluttered, making a small breeze on her back. Fairies became visible to humans for the good of the earth, nothing else. What did all this mean?

"Thanks, Evan. That's so sweet." She kissed him on the cheek.

No! Gelsey's wings flicked, and her whole body jerked upward. She did a somersault in the air and tried to steady herself. *Whoa!* She'd reacted so strongly to the horse woman showing affection to this man. How odd.

Yet, she had to stop this exchange. With all of her being, she couldn't let anything happen between the pretty horse woman and this man.

She dove toward the woman and landed in her hair. Pulling hard on the golden strands, she groaned with the exertion.

"Ouch." The woman swiped her hair, but Gelsey had already flown off. "What was that?"

She chanced a glance at the man. A small smile lifted the corners of his mouth, but he straightened and became serious. "What?"

"Something hit me on the head."

"Must have been a type of bug."

"Shall we go inside? We could have a drink in the lodge restaurant. On me?"

"I should be the one offering you a drink," the man said.

"I can see you're not yourself today."

"I think I'm very tired."

Gelsey remained suspended in the air, amazed at their similarities. She'd been feeling odd lately, too. Her instincts were wacked.

"I think a beer or glass of wine should help." The blonde handed him her helmet, took the lead rope of the horse with one hand, and grasped the man's with her other hand. They walked together, her head bending toward him to talk to him, her face too close.

Gelsey flew to them and pinched her on the elbow.

"Ouch!" She pulled away, looking around. "Something pinched my elbow."

The man spun around and stared right at her. His mouth opened in surprise. "Gelsey?"

He knew her.

He hadn't forgotten her. He must be the human she'd married for her commission in the human world. How come the magic hadn't worked to make him forget?

"Who's Gelsey?" the blonde woman asked.

"I don't know." He shook his head as though he doubted what he'd just seen.

"Let's get you inside. You've been working way too hard."

"My business is picking up though." His voice took on a more serious, controlled tone as he rattled off about his work.

The pair walked down the hill to the lodge. Gelsey struggled to remember much about him but she longed for him. Yearned to be with him and didn't want to leave. And definitely did not want the other woman to take him away.

Who was she kidding?

She was a fairy and, as such, could never be with a human.

She had a job to do. The queen and the whole of fairyhood would be disappointed if she didn't complete it. The whole earth and humankind would suffer if she failed.

Another fairy could do it. She could just be with this Evan. Forever. That's what her heart so wanted, and she didn't understand why.

Shaking her head and blinking back uncharacteristic tears, she watched the man walk away from her life. Every movement he made drew her, every expression on his face pierced her heart. He was much better than the African Wild Cat.

She came to rest on a shrub, wiping her ridiculous tears with her fingers, wrapping her wings around her so no other fairy could see.

How could the queen have allowed her to go to the human world?

Maybe she should go back to the palace and ask for more gold dust. Possibly the magic needed to be stronger. But what about him? He still would remember her. He knew something strange was going on. He'd also seen her. As a fairy.

What did it matter if he couldn't truly remember her either? Yet the heart never forgets. That was it! The heart never forgets true love!

The ground seemed to suck her in like sinking sand. Her new job and responsibilities called her, yet she couldn't leave him.

What if she lost him forever? How would her heart survive? The loneliness and restlessness that had been her portion since she'd come back to fairyland would be gone forever if she were to have him.

Impossible. Fairies and humans didn't marry.

Unless she went back into the human world.

But how?

She shook her head. Her mind was an anarchist.

She had to leave and fast. Tearing herself away from the spot, she flew up into the air, which felt like flying through water, every movement thick and difficult.

Her breathing went ragged, her throat ached, and her wings were exhausted, but she pressed on and flew into the air currents where the birds soared.

Northeastern Mpumulanga Province, here I come.

ఆ

Evan sat with a glass of wine resting on his palm, the stem fed between his fingers, and swirled it, staring in the golden liquid which mimicked the color of her wings.

He'd seen a fairy!

"I have to run." Sandy stood up. "A new group has arrived, and they want a tour of the stables so they can book some rides for the week."

"Oh, of course." He smiled as big as he could but knew she'd pick up on his falsity.

"Thanks, Evan. See you some time. Good luck with the rest of your installation."

"Appreciate it. I'm almost done. But we must keep in touch."

She nodded, her expression unsure, almost shy. She was a good girl and deserved all his attention, but he didn't know how to....

She turned and flitted out the door, neat and sexy in her jodhpurs and leather boots. Neat and sexy but not his woman.

Were there such a thing as fairies? He'd been passionate

about science all his life. There was no scientific basis for the mythological creatures. They were a figment of overactive imaginations, which it seemed he suffered from of late.

Gelsey. The name echoed in his mind. He knew her. From where? Why couldn't he place her? Where had he met a fairy? He laughed.

Oh, but she intrigued him with her almost-translucent, glowing gold wings, her chestnut hair, and brown-and-green Peter Pan outfit. A string of tiny pearls graced her creamy neck.

She'd pulled Sandy's hair and pinched her!

A smile came to his lips, and he choked back a laugh. How delightful. She was jealous.

Maybe he'd watched too much of Peter Pan years ago when he was obsessed with Julia Roberts playing the jealous Tinkerbell, being nasty to Wendy. Of course.

He took a sip of wine to ease his mind. Should he see a shrink?

No, it did seem like he'd lost his mind, but there was something more afoot. What about the fairy dust at the florist? Why did the lady know him? Where did the longing for a fairy come from? He wanted her to talk to him, to tell him what was going on. Maybe she had answers.

He didn't finish the wine as he had a job to do and a drive back to town, ten kilometers away. He paid for his and Sandy's drinks and went to his car to get his materials and tools. With concerted effort, he tried not to think of "Gelsey," but images of the sprite kept popping into his mind as he worked.

Chapter Fourteen

*G*elsey smiled at Ronald, a male fairy she worked with. He was explaining the mating habits of the giraffe in great detail.

He had a rounded, almost puffy chest as though he carried his pride around with him everywhere. But she liked his friendliness, and he'd helped her settle in the area. She'd found three mother African Wild Cats and was keeping them safe as they prepared to give birth to their kittens in the spring. At night, she would cover the entrance to their shelter with branches to keep them warm and keep predators away, a difficult task. The wild cat remained endangered from jackals and big birds of prey, but not much else. Several other animals competed for their food. She had to chase them off when they stalked small prey like dassies, field mice, and rats. The mother cats would have stronger babies if they ate many meals.

Most importantly, she had to stop them from breeding with domestic cats, except in controlled conditions.

So far, she'd been quite successful in keeping them warm, hydrated, and well fed. She wasn't sure what she would do if a human threatened them. That would be a bit harder to deal with.

With pure delight, she watched a mother cat chase a beetle around. Although pregnant, she hadn't lost her kitten-like playfulness.

A giraffe stood in the distance, its ears swiveling at any

sound in the bush. It reached up and pulled a leaf with its gummy mouth and chewed. The mate came up closer, slightly taller and more elegant.

"They're beautiful creatures. Clumsy in some ways and elegant in others," Gelsey said to Ronald. Ronald nodded and flew off to the tree near the giraffes. He bent down and flicked a nasty fly off one of the giraffe's eyelids.

A pure devotee.

She, on the other hand, was a two-faced rebel.

Yes, she loved the African Wild Cat but, at times, resented them for taking her away from her heart's desire. Yet, if it weren't for the wild cat, she wouldn't have gone on her commission to the human world in the first place.

She sat on a cool rock under the shade of a tree because, at three in the afternoon on the savannah, even in winter, the sun was hot. Spring would be here soon, but she wasn't looking forward to it—a first for her.

Ronald was sweet as were all the other fairies she'd got to know in her short time in Mpumalanga, but....

She propped her chin on her hands, her wings dipping into rest mode.

Ronald flew away to the next giraffe couple. The thing that annoyed her the most was she could never talk to another fairy for long—they were always off to do their next job, to fly off somewhere else. Sure, they cared for one another and would save each other's lives if need be, but there was no soul connection.

She struggled to get rid of the restlessness in her heart.

The cats were fine for the moment. Unable to stay moping any longer, she flew into the sky toward the conservation center, to spy on some humans. Maybe she could get a feel for how they were doing in preserving the wild cats, if anything. She hadn't seen any people around since she'd taken on her new assignment. She could get a feel for their world to find out why she wanted the man so much.

After about fifteen minutes of flying, she came to the center, a large building surrounded by smaller thatched-roof circular buildings that the South African humans called rondawels. She swooped down and perched on a windowsill of the central building and peered inside. The room looked expansive and plush, richly carpeted and furnished with dark wooden tables and chairs and a big white screen at the front. A lady laid papers down on the tables in a uniform fashion, her face pinched with concentration and worry.

Her feeling toward humans had changed. She used to despise them, even the environmentally friendly ones. This woman was helping the earth, but she was also a human with feelings. She wondered what she thought as she did a simple and boring job.

Gelsey pressed her nose against the glass and watched her with fascination. Then a man entered the room. He spoke, his gaze upon her filled with admiration. Gelsey recognized the look. Her human had given her it before.

The woman spoke, by her gestures it seemed she told him of something she was concerned about. He took her in his arms and hugged her, holding her close for a several minutes. When she pulled away, a broad smile filled her face, the frown gone. He pressed a brief kiss on her lips, making her cheeks flush, and then walked out, but not before giving her a brief wave.

She gave a little choppy return wave and went back to her job. The papers were laid out much faster, and she did a little jig around the tables.

Ah, the benefits of human love.

But it was fickle. The fairies said it didn't last, which had been the conclusion of her assignment. It seemed magical but had no staying power. The fairies aimed to find ways to make it more enduring. One day. She wouldn't be part of the second love commission. They didn't trust her to come into contact with humans too much. The queen had even stressed it in the description of her new job that she only work with them if it was essential to the wellbeing of the wild cat.

And here she was, spying on them.

She must be the naughtiest savannah fairy in Africa.

She didn't care.

It wasn't like she didn't respect her race anymore or wasn't proud of her roots. She just didn't know how to cope with the feelings inside her.

"The conference starts today," a voice spoke behind her. A fairy with lilac wings flew down and stood next to her. "It's an effort to get more sponsors for their new conservation projects."

"Oh. Hi, I'm Gelsey." She stood up and flapped her wings in greeting.

"I'm Birdy."

Gelsey laughed.

"I know. I don't know why my mother fairy gave me the name. She wasn't thinking straight—had too much dandelion wine the night the queen's servants dropped me off. I come all the way from Swaziland by the way."

"Pleased to meet you."

Gelsey peered through the window again, not wanting to miss any more exchanges between the man and woman.

"Are you helping with their conservation program?"

Gelsey turned to give her attention to the fairy, realizing she might look a bit odd, being so intent on meaningless human activity. "I'm helping the African Wild Cat. Do you know if they're talking about it at the conference?"

"I don't think so."

"Oh." She pretended disappointment. Her ability to lie had come with her from the human world—well, not lie so much as hide her true feelings because they were dangerous and rather treasonous.

"I thought you would know if you're watching them so closely. Come away," the fairy urged, tugging her on the arm.

"Okay."

"Fly with me. I found an injured wild cat a few days ago. Let me take you to him."

"Really?" Gelsey should be upset, but all she felt was weariness. Her wings didn't want to straighten right away, but she forced them open and took flight with the other fairy.

While in the air, Birdy spoke in a hushed tone. "Have you touched the silver dust?"

"No." Gelsey was all ears. "Why?"

"You act like it. My uncle fairy touched the silver dust by accident. He was never the same again. He saw things. Strange things."

"Like what?"

"I'm not supposed to tell you, but, well, you need to be warned."

Gelsey became quiet and continued to fly with Birdy, strength filling her again as she soared above the earth. Lately, she'd enjoyed flight more than her work on earth. She felt free, above everything, and had time to think through things. She often flew higher than the other fairies just to get away from their constant chatter and activity.

"He perceived thoughts and ideas about the universe fairies don't understand. He saw into another realm. I can't explain because he never went into detail, but he became strange. He would watch humans all the time. He didn't work as hard yet seemed to believe strongly about the strangest things."

"How odd. What is the silver dust for, then? If it makes fairies go bad, why do they keep it?"

"The queen uses the silver dust on humans, not fairies. Only she and some select royal servants are allowed to use it."

"But I thought she used gold dust on humans."

"When has she ever done that?" Birdy became indignant and jerked her head up at Gelsey who flew above her.

Gelsey didn't feel like bringing up her past commission, but the tense silence from Birdy made her speak. "I used it for my commission in the human world."

"You're *that* fairy."

"That fairy?"

"The one who came back from the human world. But I heard you were nearly lost to them."

What could she say? An ache filled her gut, seeming to

bloom inside her like a wild plant or a grapevine in summer. They'd betrayed her. Unwittingly, yes, but the betrayal cut deep. She'd come back to the fairy world because she saw no hope for her human existence. She had a duty to fulfill as a fairy to the earth.

Why did it hurt so much to do what was right?

Or had she?

She'd abandoned a human she loved. Did he feel the emptiness and restlessness she struggled with every day? Was he unable to find joy in the simple tasks he'd previously enjoyed? Was he always questioning, wondering, confused?

Saving the wild cat would help the earth. But humans were part of the earth, too. By abandoning him, was she harming the earth?

Fairies believed in the queen. They obeyed her without question most of the time. If there were any disputes, she often reasoned with them. She had a power to convince anyone to her way of thinking. Since her return, she'd questioned the queen's wisdom in bringing her back to the fairy world.

If she could find a way to return to the human world, would she be happy again? Would everything fall into place? Or would she long for her fairyhood?

She flew faster.

"Wait. You're going the wrong way," Birdy said, her long black hair in a stream behind her.

Gelsey turned around. "I'm sorry. I get carried away up in the sky."

"Should have been a sky fairy."

She shook her head. "Odd that. Aren't we all sky fairies?"

Birdy ignored her. She had become too philosophical. The pretty fairy took a dive toward earth and Gelsey followed. They came to a clump of trees. Lying next to one of the trees was the cat, barely alive. Gelsey stroked its head, shocked at how cold his fur felt.

"I'll leave you, then." Birdy buzzed up and waved to her.

"Okay."

She disappeared before Gelsey could ask any questions. She didn't even know what type of fairy Birdy was.

The cat's eyes were closed, but he purred gently to comfort his own distress. If it survived, she would have to lead him to where the other wild cats were so he could breed. Was it worth it?

She spent some time with the cat, stroking him and tending to his wounds.

Gold dust would go down well. Or silver dust. What did silver dust do? Could silver dust help her? She needed answers, and maybe silver dust would help her see. Where could she get hold of some without traveling all the way to the palace?

Chapter Fifteen

"Do you believe in fairies?" Evan sat opposite Marissa in a coffee shop two stores down from her florist. He held a coffee mug in his hand while the heat burnt his skin but helped distract him from the pain of making an absolute fool of himself.

Marissa smiled but held no ridicule in her expression. "I don't think so. But at the moment, I don't believe in logic alone."

"Me, too."

"Why did you bring me here to talk to me about fairies?"

"The glitter you have. Maybe it's to do with a fairy." He paused, taking in a deep breath. "I saw a fairy a week ago. I know I wasn't imagining it because she pinched a friend of mine who felt the pain."

"Are you sure it wasn't a strange bug?"

"I've never seen a bug with startling green eyes, beautiful chestnut curls, and a small pointy nose."

"Wings?" Marissa took a sip of her tea, her face a picture of calm despite the crazy conversation.

"Golden wings that sparkled in the sun."

"Very romantic."

"I'm being serious. And I knew her name."

Marissa nodded. "What?"

"Gelsey."

Marissa stared at him. "I know that name."

"The gold dust. Do you still have it?"

"I won't part with it. After I touched it when you came in the shop, I obtained some new big regular clients. And a gorgeous man asked me on a date."

"So, it's magic. I knew it."

"You can't take it away from me. It's mine." She stared at him, firmness in her voice, yet no malice.

He raised his eyebrow. "You were offering me some for my flower arrangement."

"Before I realized it's magic."

"It must be connected to the fairy."

She shrugged. "Your idea's a bit too bizarre. Fairies are from childhood stories."

"And gold dust isn't?"

She slid her finger along the rim of the teacup as if in deep thought. "If this fairy appearance is true, what am I to do about it?"

"I'm not sure. May I just touch the gold dust once? Maybe it will help me to find answers."

"If you do find answers"—Marissa sighed and pushed her cup away—"please tell me. As much as I like this goodness coming my way, I'd like to know what's going on. It plays with my mind when I'm in bed at night, trying to fall asleep. I'm tampering with magic and have no idea how it works. It's scary."

Evan nodded. She needn't know he'd been having the same sleepless hours. All she needed was clarity, just like him.

He gulped down his coffee, and Marissa led him to the cramped florist shop to dip his fingers into a velvet-covered cardboard box with gold glitter inside. His life had gone way out of control, and he knew it could only be love. And he had it bad.

ଓ

Gelsey rested her head against her makeshift pillow inside her new home in a cave. The cave was hidden behind a small waterfall near the wild cat area. Exhausted, she hummed to herself, trying to rest, but sleep refused to come. As much as her whole body and wings ached from pulling the wild cat to a safer area, she couldn't sleep. At least Ronald had helped her. Being a male fairy, he had more arm strength. But his brawn hadn't been enough for the animal. They'd had to enlist five other fairies to bring the cat to safety.

The creature lay in an enclosed area covered in a tangle of vegetation, fast asleep. Its wounds were clean and sealed with fairy bandages made of flower petals dipped in gum tree sap. She'd even found the cat a few tiny fish from the river to eat. He'd taken several small bites and gulped down some water in desperation. He would survive and eventually flourish. He had a fighting spirit.

Tending the cat got her thinking. Her new job was special. She loved caring for the cats, but any fairy could do her job. What was so out of the ordinary about it? Fairies didn't go to school like humans. Instead, they were mentored by older fairies while they helped with simple tasks. It had been drummed into her growing up that the basic expectation of fairyhood was enthusiasm and sacrifice. She'd lost her enthusiasm and wondered if she could sacrifice all anymore.

Humans suffered from depression, so maybe she was still human inside. She needed fairy dust, gold or silver, to break the spell, and only the queen could help her.

Dreams came to her in the night. Human dreams. Strange sensations on her body—a man touching her in places a human would be aware of, bringing intense pleasure she'd never known before as a fairy. She awoke with her eyes wide, unable to process the images.

Closing her eyes, she forced herself to sleep and eventually dropped off again.

More dreams haunted her. She fell down a dark tunnel and couldn't stop. Grasping at the sides, her fingers became raw. She didn't have wings to buoy her up from the fall. Instead, she plummeted deeper and deeper into the darkness, the light above her becoming a tiny speck. Then she landed softly on a surface of great comfort. Fumbling for something, anything to help her know where she was, she found a small ball. She squeezed the ball and awoke.

What did it all mean?

As dawn seeped gray light into the cave, Gelsey woke up, her eyes gritty and half glued-shut, but she had to get going at the first break of dawn. She flew to Ronald's home, a hundred meters from her own.

"Please, Ronald," she pleaded with him. "Look after my cats for me. Just for four days. I'm going to the palace. I have to."

He nodded. "I know."

She didn't even ask how he knew. It must have been pretty obvious she was in serious trouble.

The journey proved grueling. She flew the whole day and part of the night the first day. The second day progressed slower as her energy waned, but she pressed on. Late in the evening, she reached the palace, lit by candlelight and fireflies at night.

She requested an audience with the queen. Her request was granted without question. Surely, she didn't look that bad.

While she waited, drinks and food were brought to her, and attendants offered her a place to rest. She smiled. They remembered her, but she didn't deserve this treatment. She'd failed as a fairy.

Before she'd even finished a little food, she was summoned to the queen's living room—another privilege she didn't deserve.

"Come in, Gelsey." The queen sounded serious, and everything within her wanted to run and hide, but she couldn't escape from the turmoil within any longer.

"What can I do for you?" She offered Gelsey a seat and took another one opposite her.

Gelsey ignored the strong authority and power oozing from her. She would not be intimidated. Looking around at the softly lit room decorated in pinks, greens, and blues, she remembered waking up from her human commission in the very same spot, relieved it was all over. How wrong she'd been.

"The magic didn't work."

"What magic?"

The queen didn't know? "The gold dust. It didn't take all my memories away. I'm troubled by thoughts, dreams...desires. I can't let go of my human love."

The queen rose and walked to the other end of the room, placing her fingers on the jars for the gold and silver dust. She was going to bring some more dust. Maybe it would all be over soon. She came back to her empty-handed, making Gelsey's wings sag into a crumpled mess at her back.

"So, it's stronger than I thought. That's good."

"What?" She so wanted to shout at the queen's quiet, unhurried manner. Was she so oblivious to the confusion inside of her?

"The human love. It's very strong. It means the human race will survive. My experiment worked."

"Experiment? So, I was just part of an experiment?"

The queen sighed. "You're a fairy and always will be at heart. A fairy's life purpose is to sacrifice herself for the earth. You should know that."

"I don't want to be a fairy."

"It won't be any easier to be a human. You will have to sacrifice yourself for your job and your family."

"I'm willing to do that. I know he's suffering. I don't think a human should suffer, too. I don't only care for the wild cats."

"By becoming human, you won't relieve his suffering. You may increase it because you have to tell him the truth—how the dust made him love you and how you deceived him. He might not trust you. He could turn against you. Then you will be all alone in a world you don't belong in."

Gelsey gave a tight laugh. The queen had described her current feelings, but she wouldn't understand. "I want to take the chance. Even if it kills me, I can't abandon him any longer."

The queen looked down, her face taut. "Then I cannot stop you. I ask you one thing. If you go, please help the wild cats somehow. That's all I ask. And keep your smile." She touched her cheeks and tears pricked Gelsey's eyes. The queen did care and so did the other fairies in their own way.

Maybe she was being selfish, but there was no other way. "I will help them. I promise."

"You're a good fairy. I'm sorry this has happened, but you have made the ultimate sacrifice for your race. I hope you will be rewarded in the earth."

The queen picked up her wand that shimmered with silver dust. She shook it over Gelsey's head. Silver glitter came raining down upon her before she had a moment to blink.

This time it wasn't a dream. She fell down a dark tunnel but without sides. Grasping for something to cling onto, she just floundered and tumbled out of control. But she fell toward a light. The light grew brighter, louder, and harsher until she reached it with a jerk.

Oh, she hadn't been falling but rather soaring upward into something.

Chapter Sixteen

*E*van stood in the florist shop with his fingers inside the tiny box. The gold dust tickled them yet seemed impossible to hold. What made it so ticklish was the sensation of not feeling something you could see. Then a strange tingling went up his arm and took over his whole body. He closed his eyes, more out of fear than anything else. What if the magic was bad? When he opened his eyes, he wasn't surprised to find her standing in front of him but in human form. Memories came crashing down, so strong he held his head in his hands to relieve the pressure. She was Gelsey, his wife, the woman with whom he'd shared the most intimate and beautiful times of his life. He was married to the woman standing in front of him who looked almost identical to the fairy who'd pinched Sandy, sans the wings and Tinkerbell outfit.

"Evan."

Her tone told him she'd missed him and longed for him. But he stood still, reeling, wanting answers.

Glancing at Marissa, he knew she remained quiet not because of shock or even surprise, but because she knew it best to do so.

"Gelsey. Where have you been?"

"I have to explain. It's a long story."

"I'm as ready as I'll ever be." He choked the words out, afraid of what she would tell him.

"I can hear it later." Marissa touched Evan's arm. "Why don't you go for another cup of coffee?"

He nodded at Marissa. "Thanks. And keep the gold glitter in a safe place."

"What?" Gelsey noticed the box and snatched it away. "Where did you get this?" Her voice came out sharper than usual.

"I kept some from when you showered it all over Evan."

"Oh." She stared at the woman. Some strong emotion clouded her face. "I see." She handed it back to Marissa. "Use it sparingly on yourself. No one else." She gripped Marissa's hand and gave it a frantic squeeze then pulled away.

Marissa nodded, her eyes brimming with emotion.

Evan walked out the room, hoping Gelsey would follow. She was beautiful, and he longed to touch her, but everything inside him screamed *How can I trust her. Who is she? Will she disappear again?*

Those few frantic days of searching for her had come back to him in full force. The reason he'd been at the top of Signal Hill with a flashlight. The police car had been for the officer who helped him with the search. The fear and despair had been all-consuming. He'd convinced himself he could never love or even enjoy life again until he found her. He'd already lost his twin sister to a horrible sports accident and then he'd lost the woman of his dreams. Having his heart ripped out twice in one lifetime was enough for him.

She'd done that to him. She'd disappeared without a trace and then she'd wiped his memory of her forever. Until today. He needed to know the reason.

How could she have done it? Could she be using her magic powers to manipulate him, to play with him? He gritted his teeth as he walked toward the coffee shop so fast Gelsey had to run to keep up with him.

Once they were seated, before the waitress even took their orders, he spoke. "What's going on, Gelsey? Why are you playing with my life, messing me around like this?"

"Please, let me explain from the beginning."

"You'd better have a very good reason. I searched for you for days. Marissa and I were frantic. Are you a witch?"

"I'm a human. I used to be a fairy."

"And you will chop and change from one to another whenever you like?"

"I chose to lose my fairyhood to become a human to be with you." Her eyes held tears. They glittered in the dim light of the coffee shop.

She used her tears to manipulate him. He bit his lip to stop from swearing. Had she left him for someone else but then the relationship had turned sour so she'd come back to him? He still doubted the whole fairy thing—way too fanciful.

The waitress came to take their orders, and he tried to sound polite and not choked and angry. His one fist ached from gripping the chair on which he sat.

"Who are you?" he demanded, the waitress barely out of hearing.

"I was commissioned by the African Savannah Queen Fairy to come to the human world for one year, to marry a man, and experience human love."

"I don't understand."

Her explanation sounded like same crazy story made up by someone who'd read too many fantasy novels. Yet, his vision of her pinching Sandy, who'd felt the pain, kept him open-minded.

"The queen needed a fairy to experience human love to help save the earth. Certain humans aren't having enough children— the good humans, the ones who care for the earth. She chose me and promised me the best job ever if I succeeded in finding out why. I was to come back and report what I'd gleaned. She gave me gold fairy dust to sprinkle on a single man who cared for the environment. So I was changed into a human, and a fairy, Ziana, helped me set up a job in the human world."

Yes, he'd intended to buy flowers for Sandy, but then Gelsey had sprinkled gold dust on him. Exactly when his compulsion to be with her had begun. Her story could explain his bizarre behavior.

"What did sprinkling the gold dust do to me?"

"It made you want to marry me."

Evan pulled back. It all made sense. His love for Gelsey had been false. It had been the product of fairy magic. Who would have thought? Was this all a crazy dream and he would wake up one day, the same man from before, plodding along, surviving but not experiencing excruciating pain and betrayal? But no, she was real, and he'd just found out she'd used him.

"So, that's why I was crazy enough to marry a girl a few days after meeting her? I thought you were just so right for me I couldn't resist you."

She was crying, but he didn't care. "I thought so, too."

"But you knew the magic?"

"I fell in love with you. Being with you, the time we had together. I hated the human world at first, but you made me happy. I didn't want to lose you, so I went to meet Ziana to try to negotiate with her, to find a way. She saw my confusion and pain and thought I needed to finish my commission early. They didn't want to lose me. I had a big job to do—to save the Wild Cats. She convinced me I had no guarantee you would love me once the magic was gone. So, I left to get away from the confusion and pain."

"And left me with it?"

"They assured me you wouldn't remember anything about me and vice versa. I knew it was for the best for both of us."

"How can you assume that?"

"I was scared. They convinced me. I had to follow my duty."

She'd chosen duty over love. She hadn't believed in them enough to stay. Yet, how could she believe in them if she knew what they had was based on magic, not real love?

He couldn't speak. Thankfully, their coffees arrived and he drank down the bitter liquid that scalded his throat. Two coffees today and he didn't even like coffee. Punishing himself didn't diminish the arrows piercing his heart with each new revelation.

"Please, let me explain what happened next."

He nodded, unable to look at her. Instead, he focused on the artwork on the walls of the café.

"I went back into the fairy world and forgot about you for a while, but I wasn't happy. I was restless. I couldn't sleep at night, and I felt lonely. The crazy thing is fairies don't feel isolated. We don't have the same emotions as humans. Our life work is our love. We have friends but not soul mates. You were my soul mate, and something inside me craved you."

His gaze landed on her, and she looked away. She took a few sips of her drink and swallowed down some tears. He took a hanky from his pocket for her. She didn't need to look like a sobbing child at a restaurant.

"This is hard, Evan."

He nodded but refused to make it any easier. He needed to see how genuine she was. Bringing on tears meant nothing. He wanted to know the truth and her reasoning. He was a logical man and had lost that strength when Gelsey had sprinkled gold dust on him. He didn't plan on losing it again and then losing his heart with it.

"When I found you with Sandy on the field, I remembered you. Not so much how you looked, but your heart. A heart never forgets the one they love."

"Go on."

"I was on my way to my new job to save the Wild Cats in the Kruger National Park when I saw you. I had to go because I had my job to do, and what else *could* I do? I was a fairy and you were a human."

"What about the magic?"

"I don't have access to the magic. Only the queen does."

Something moved inside of him—a tiny bit of forgiveness and understanding came through. Had she been a victim of this cruel experiment just as much as he? Yet, she could have chosen not to go through with it. Shouldn't she have told him the truth earlier on?

No, their love was a farce. He couldn't stay married to a

woman he didn't really know. She was a fairy. She'd grown up in a different background to him. What did they have in common anymore? What human had ever fallen in love with a fairy before? What were fairies like? The only fairy he had any knowledge of was the mischievous Tinkerbell, and she wasn't real.

"What did you do?" His tone came out softer.

Her shoulders slumped in weariness, but she continued. "I tried to work in my new job, but the loneliness and restless feelings increased. I knew I couldn't finish my task. A fairy's goal in life is self-sacrifice and enthusiasm. Sure, I'd sacrificed my happiness for my fairy job, but I lacked enthusiasm. I wasn't right for the position anymore. And I wanted to come back here, to be with you. To be with the man I love and who loves me."

Did he love her? She was a stranger to him. He had no assurance of her honesty.

"How can we make this work, Gelsey? Our love was a farce. I can't trust you."

"Our love wasn't a farce. Your love was genuine, and so was mine. It transcended realms. It went beyond the magic."

Her green gaze pierced him. He couldn't breathe at the intensity within it. Too much to process. She spoke a fairy tale to him, not real life.

"I can't promise you the same love as before. Everything has changed."

"Won't you give us a chance? We can work on it. We can start from the beginning."

She cried out to him, and he hated turning her away, but he needed time. Maybe she was genuine, but she'd lied to him—she was a different breed. What was a fairy? A type of animal, a spirit being? He couldn't fathom bridging the differences between them, so suddenly, as if they were back to their lives before. As if nothing had come between them.

"I can't do this yet. I need to think about us, about you."

She looked down and stirred her coffee, staring into the caramel liquid. She'd hardly touched it.

"I'll take it slowly. I'm very patient." She spoke, the pleading gone, but he knew it was her last stab in the dark.

He sighed, plonking his empty cup down, the bitter taste remaining in his mouth. "I can't, Gelsey. Not yet."

She nodded but kept her head down. The hanky came to her nose and she blew. Shiny, chestnut hair cascaded down her back and shoulders. He'd suspected she wasn't real before—so beautiful and vulnerable, yet strong and determined. Deep inside, he'd known their love had been too good to be true.

"I'll come fetch my stuff. I'm wearing the same clothes I wore when I left the human world, and I have a key for the house in my handbag. Shall I return it to you afterward?"

"I'll let you find a place first. I don't want to kick you out on the street."

"I'll manage." She squared her shoulders, yet glimmers of her broken heart and dashed hopes shone through.

"No. It's not right. What do you know about finding a place? About the world?" Her glaring naivety made perfect sense.

"You taught me much." She rose up, taking a R50 note out of her handbag and placed it on the table. "Thanks for the drink." She'd paid way too much for a drink she hadn't touched.

She walked out the café, her soft steps scraping deep furrows of guilt into him. As much as he hated to see her in so much pain, he couldn't give her his all. Not yet. It was for the best for both of them. They were unable to depend on the magic anymore.

Chapter Seventeen

Gelsey had no idea what to do with herself. She walked out the coffee shop before she burst into a fit of weeping in front of all the customers and Evan. Ambling down the lane, she held back the sobs with everything within her. She needed to go back to Marissa and check if she still had a job. If anything, she needed to cope in the human world. Survival was all she could hang onto—not happiness. She hadn't told Evan all the truth. A very small part of her, the part that wanted to keep strong, was relieved he hadn't jumped at it straight away because she'd seen a very scary thing at the florist earlier. If it was true, their love was false in every sense. She'd tried to remain positive while talking to him to convince him to give them a chance, but the uncertainty eroded all her hope away.

She needed to find out if what she'd seen was true.

"Hi." She came up to Marissa buried in some books.

"Gelsey. I'm so glad you're safe." Marissa came around her counter and wrapped her in a heart-warming hug, bringing some sanity back into her.

"I was so worried about you." Marissa wiped some tears from her eyes and sniffled. "We searched everywhere and the scariest thing is, all of a sudden, we both forgot about you as if you'd never existed. Where have you been?

"It's so hard to explain. I was a fairy and was sent to the

human world for a commission."

"I knew you were magic. I even told Evan, but he wouldn't believe me. Well, at first."

"You're very perceptive."

"The gold dust and your innocence and the chemistry between you and Evan all made it clear to me. Where is he?"

"I'm going to move out. I just need to find a place first."

"What? No. Don't destroy my only hope in life that true love still exists. I had begun to believe in magic after all." Her eyes shone, pricking Gelsey with more guilt for letting her friend's idealism collapse.

She shook her head, the sadness resting on her like heavy frost on grass. "I know I asked you to put the gold dust away, but may I see it? I need to check something."

"Sure. It was yours, and I stole it. I should give it back to you."

She shook her head. "You need some magic in your life. I can't do anything with it anymore."

Marissa opened the lid with such reverence, and Gelsey took a few sprinkles out, laying them on her palm. She sucked in a breath that felt as cold as ice though the day wasn't particularly cold. "I knew it."

"What?"

"You won't understand. But it's all over. There's no hope for our love to work because it was never love in the first place."

"That's nonsense." Marissa's eyes were fire, her face flushed. She pressed her finger into Gelsey's chest. "I don't care what spell or potion or dust was used to get Evan interested in you in the beginning, but you got yourself one of the best guys in the world who treated you like a true gem. I don't think it had anything to do with magic but good old-fashioned passion and love. If you give up on him, you're the stupidest woman in the world."

Marissa pulled away, seeming embarrassed by her outburst. "Now, I have to finish this paperwork." She took in a deep breath and smiled. "I expect to hear good news from you in a few weeks because I think you love him just as much. Whatever you gave up for him must have been intense. I can see it all over your face. If you're willing to sacrifice it for him, then I'm sure you're capable of fighting for him with every ounce of your being."

"Thanks." Gelsey touched the top of her friend's hand which already wrote out an order form in a tight scribble. "Can I have my job back?"

"You never lost it in the first place."

"You're the best. I'm going to buy you...."

"Enough of that. Seeing as you want your job back, I have lots for you to do." She turned all serious. "Could you change the window display and dust the shop? Then I need five flower arrangements for a wedding. I haven't had a chance to do anything since you disappeared."

Gelsey walked to the back to get a duster and some cleaning materials with a small smile on her face. Marissa had a way of bringing stability to her yo-yo emotions. She set to work, glad to have a distraction from the pain and crazy thoughts pumping through her.

Worries kept intruding though.

She'd found silver dust mixed in with the gold. The queen had mixed them, which meant she'd had it all along. That's why she could never forget Evan. It wasn't because their love was stronger than the magic. She'd touched the silver dust when she'd sprinkled it on Evan. If an ordinary fairy touched silver dust, she would see things from all realms—or so Birdy had explained to her. She would never be the same again. It explained her connection to the human world when she went back for her new job. Not because she loved Evan.

Yet, how come she never saw fairies when she was human before? This was all so confusing.

She figured because she'd touched the silver dust, she would see things as a human other humans didn't see. She would see hidden fairies or spiritual things. If only she could see what held Evan back. His words had made sense, but if his love was as strong as Marissa had said, then he would see past their differences and make it work.

How could she convince him if she was unsure herself?

ભ

Evan came home to find Gelsey's belongings still in the house. So, that's why the house had felt so empty the last few weeks. Gelsey's things had been gone. She had disappeared. So, the vast emptiness in his heart and his crazy behavior hadn't been because of Trisha or because he'd gone mad.

Gelsey had returned but not home yet. Marissa had probably given the woman her job back. She was like that.

He couldn't kick her out, yet what could he say or do to her when she arrived? He walked into the kitchen to find some food, although he didn't feel hungry.

Why hadn't he followed his instincts and questioned her in the beginning when he'd first discovered how few possessions she owned? He'd trusted her foolishly because of some stupid fairy dust.

Fairies. They were real, and they had a strange modus operandi—playing with people's lives and emotions for the good of the earth. What about caring about people?

What exactly had Gelsey gone through? She'd known their entire time together she would have to leave him. How could she have given her whole heart to him knowing she would leave him forever? Why hadn't she said something? Her duty had proven stronger than her love for him.

He took out a pan and heated some butter, then broke an egg into the pan once it was hot. He popped a slice of bread in the toaster and set the kettle on to make some tea. One egg wouldn't do it, but he didn't have the energy to think of anything else to eat.

The sound of a key turning in the lock made every muscle in his body stiffen.

She came straight into the kitchen. "Hi." She glanced at him then set her bag down. She took out a mug and plopped a teabag inside just like everything was normal and every day, like she wasn't this strange mythological creature who lived in his home, dressed as a human.

The kettle bubbled on its last effort, and Gelsey topped off their mugs. She finished her tea, grabbed her drink, and went out the room. The emptiness felt stark. Just making tea, she'd infused a presence in the room that pierced his soul.

He wanted to know about her. What did she do as a kid? What did kid fairies do? What did she like?

Why did she leave him?

Didn't she know he couldn't take it? He'd told her about Trisha, shared his pain from her death, how much it had affected him throughout his life. Yet she'd still gone. The few days she'd been missing, his heart had been held in a vise grip of fear so strong, it almost strangled the life out of him. He'd somehow managed to continue the search for her without collapsing or going to the hospital. Some moments, the chest pain had been so severe, he was convinced he would land six feet under.

After his egg was cooked and on the toast on top of a plate, he went through to the living room. He needed some space to think, but Gelsey sat there as he expected, leafing through the property section of the newspaper.

"Rentals are expensive," he said. "I'll find something for you. One of my clients might be able to help you."

"No, Evan. I need to stand on my own."

"It's my fault you're a human now."

She gave a bitter laugh. "I don't know whose fault it is. It just is, and I have to make the most of my life."

She said it with such sadness. He went to her and took her hand, unable to see her like this. "I wish I could promise you forever."

"Me, too." She looked up at him, her eyes flooded with tears again. "I'm sorry. I've been doing lots of crying today. Makes up for all those years of frivolous fairyhood."

"What do you mean?"

"Fairies don't cry much. We're happy most of the time. We

get frustrated and tired but not often. We also don't feel much. Don't care much."

"I thought you were self-sacrificial."

"It's all for the earth. Yeah, sure, we kept each other safe, and we would lay down our lives for each other. It's not that I'm not proud of my roots. I was a good fairy. I helped the earth greatly. I helped domestic cats and insects. I was helping the African Wild Cat when I left. It's close to extinction."

"Would the earth fall to pieces without your race?"

"Yes, of course." Her face lit with certainty.

He suppressed a smile and found himself squeezing her hand. Shocked, he pulled back, not wishing to get too near to this strange yet so familiar creature. At such close range, his gaze roamed her blouse and sculpted trousers. He remembered her human form very well—many beautiful parts of it. His body betrayed his mind and his pants tightened. Oh, she had the softest skin in the world. And her hair. He could run his fingers through it for hours, place his face inside its mass and take the scent in, drink it in as if it were food. Today he knew why it was the most unusual color he'd even seen. She wasn't fully human. Never would be in his eyes. But how could he let go and forget being used?

He looked down at the soggy egg and stuffed a mouthful in.

"Looks like you've been missing my cooking."

"I'll manage."

He ate in silence, increasing the space between them to give his mind the freedom to think without being pulled by the sudden attraction for her he'd forgotten. Since she'd gone missing, he hadn't thought much of the powerful sexual energy between them. He'd only thought of finding the woman he loved. The sexual energy had nothing to do with the magic and all to do with her curvy body, the way she spoke softly yet with certainty, the way she carried herself with lightness, grace and poise, and the mischievous twinkle in her eyes at times. The list went on.

Oh, he'd missed her.

She was still the same energy, the same source of feminine

food for him. No, he had to be sensible. He'd be unable to handle it if she left again. Who was she? Could he trust her?

She pressed the remote to turn the TV on. He covered his mouth to hide a smile. Gelsey had loved TV before she'd disappeared. He understood for the first time the screen was her way of learning about the human world.

"What conclusion did you come to with the queen?"

"I'm sorry?" She snapped out of her trance and looked at him, a deep frown blanketing her eyes.

"What did you tell the queen about human love?"

"Um...." She seemed reticent to speak, appearing serious, more solemn than he'd ever known her. She had changed since she'd disappeared. Her face was drawn and more mature. "I told her it's hard to be human, but love holds families together and makes them strong. It's the foundation for having a family. She concluded human love is fickle and doesn't last. I couldn't disagree with her. It seemed from what I'd seen in this world, it doesn't often last. Yet, I believed ours could have."

"Do you still believe?"

"I don't know. I'm afraid. I also wonder if the magic made it work, and do we have what it takes?"

"Oh. I thought you were all eager to continue as we left off?"

"How naïve do you think I am?"

"Not as naïve as you were. Seems like pain has matured you."

She jerked her head toward him but nodded. Flickers of pain crossed her face. There seemed to be lines there that hadn't been there before. He wanted to reach out to her, to squeeze her hand or hug her, but held back.

"Do you hate your queen for doing this to you?"

She was silent for a long time, sipping her tea. "I don't hate her, but I don't understand her thinking either. I won't ever understand because I'm not a fairy anymore. I stopped being a proper fairy after I married you. It changed me."

"Do you think she meant for this to happen?"

"No." She shook her head. "I think she underestimated the

power of what would happen."

"The power of love?"

Gelsey looked at him, light entering her eyes, but then they became shadowed again.

She was withdrawing, and he hadn't made it any easier. Where was the certainty she seemed to hold in the coffee shop, trying to convince him to give them a second chance? Maybe she'd also realized it wasn't as straightforward as before.

"What did you do as a kid?"

"What?"

"I mean a child fairy. What do you call them?"

"A faye, a bud, whatever. I used to help my mother fairy guide bees and butterflies. Where we stayed, there were too many bees. We were trying to move them to other areas to ensure an even distribution."

"Didn't they sting you?"

"We didn't upset them. We enticed them."

"Ah. Tell me how." He imagined her as a little fairy, flying from flower to flower, chasing bees and getting up to all sorts of mischief.

She smiled. "It's a long story."

"I have all night."

Gelsey began her story and didn't stop. Evan put his empty plate down, rested his hands against the back of the sofa, and listened, his gaze upon her face, drinking in each nuance of movement as she spoke, each little gesture as she grew animated with details. He learned more about her in the hours while they spoke that evening than in the first few months of their marriage.

He was falling for her all over again.

This time, it was for real. Although, he began to think it had always been real.

He wanted to trust her. More and more, he wanted to let go and let the love happen again.

Chapter Eighteen

Gelsey woke up with the first bird chirping outside the window. No sunlight shone yet as it was the end of winter and the nights were still long. She was deep under the duvet with Evan lying next to her but no part of his body touching hers. He'd gone to sleep on the couch, saying she should take the bed. They'd stayed up until one in the morning, talking about her childhood. It felt so good to be honest with him and share every part of her life. There were no longer secrets, yet she had little hope of the romance reviving. He didn't want to touch her. He held back, and she didn't feel the magic as before.

When had he come into the bed? At least she hadn't hogged his bed all to herself. She didn't belong here, using his stuff, eating his food, and burning his electricity. She should find her own place, but lying here, warm in the bed, doing nothing for a change felt so good. Her life had been busy the last few weeks as a fairy and then the trauma of coming back to the human world to find she would be facing it on her own, had knocked her body into an exhausted state. She stared at the ceiling fan, which splashed a pronged shadow against the ceiling, and sighed.

Sleep eluded her no matter how much she needed it.

Turning quietly so as not to wake him, she faced her husband. Yes, she was still married to him. Visible in the faint light from a streetlight outside, his bangs looked fluffy against his forehead, his face serene. His chest rose and fell with the steady breathing of sleep. His lips were flat and shaped just right. Good kissing lips. They'd caused her body to do strange and wonderful things when he pressed them against hers. Okay, so maybe the magic hadn't gone totally.

Her whole body tingled with longing to touch him, to feel his warmth upon her, enveloping her, to mingle with him, his lips, his male hardness inside of her, his fervent hands upon her breasts, upon her back, upon her buttocks.

A shaky sigh escaped her. He opened his eyes as if he knew her thoughts and stared right at her, almost into her.

"Oh," she said.

Before she could ask him why he'd come to the bed, he moved closer and covered her lips with his. Although his mouth was dry from a night under warm covers, they were soon moistened by their movement together. Powerful surges of energy came to her as he kissed. He pressed himself against her and grasped for her breast. Under his careful hands, her body responded with perfect bliss. Satisfaction threaded through her with each movement, satisfaction yet hunger for more. He fumbled through the layers of clothing until he found her bare breast and fiddled with the nipple between his fingers. All confusion and doubts fled in the height he brought her to with this simple movement and his teasing kisses. She kissed him back hard, with longing like a powerful force to make them as one again. It had been way too long.

Soon his hand was on her other breast. She arched her pelvis toward him and felt the familiar yet long-missed sensation of his hardness against her. He pulled away to remove his clothing, and she did the same. Too bad where this would take them. Too bad about the possible confusion it would bring. Her body needed this closeness, needed the release, the joy he could bring.

They were naked and against each other, and she let out a cry. He mumbled something inaudible in response. No barriers remained between their skin, and she soared higher than the sky. She engulfed his lips, tasting their sweetness as he pressed into her slowly yet with strength. She arched back and forth, bringing him to climax first, but she followed soon afterward as he played with her breasts. She collapsed in his arms, exhausted but at peace.

Until she analyzed where this would take them.

The cold made her shiver, so she put her clothes back on and lay to face the window, away from him, to calm her thoughts and reduce the intensity of the moment. She still didn't want to get up even though the birds were awake and the sun announced the day.

A small tremble flickered through her as he wrapped his arms around her waist and pulled her toward him in a spooning position. The simple affection took her breath away and brought tears to her eyes.

She responded by stroking his arms, his hairs sweet male friction under her palm.

Oh, it felt good to be back in his arms.

Where to? Could she risk giving him her heart? What if he pushed her away?

She dozed, the security of his closeness easing the exhaustion of her body into blessed sleep.

ᣓ

Evan awoke late to open his factory. He had an installation in half an hour, too. His heart rising to his throat in panic at the lack of time, he pulled away from Gelsey and ran to the shower. As he stood under the hot spray, washing off the soap, he went through his actions from the night before.

He'd tried to fall asleep on the coach but knowing the sexiest woman alive slept in his bed had made the tension unbearable. He'd considered jacking off to relieve the tension, but the idea had seemed so useless to him. That's what he'd done since Gelsey had gone missing, and it had done nothing to satisfy his real sexual needs. Or maybe it ran deeper than a simple release.

He craved her body. How could he have thought she could just go out of his life? Yes, she'd betrayed him, although he was beginning to understand her more and more. She'd acted according to her nature—her fairy nature. But even her personality had started to change. Being with him had changed her. *He* had changed her. His love had been strong enough to make her give up her whole heritage. She had no guarantees he would reciprocate her love, but she'd taken the chance. Her actions spoke volumes to him of her determination and self-sacrifice. She wasn't a fairy anymore, but he knew the woman he'd married was special beyond magic. Pushing those thoughts away, he'd tried to sleep. Then thoughts of her body had intruded into his mind. The curve of her breasts as they dipped in to her waist sharply, and the beautiful elements topped with perfect, taut pink nipples ready for him to touch, to taste, and to pleasure.

The rounded curve of her abdomen was pure liquid gold to run his hand down until he reached the pinnacle of her beauty— the garden enclosed with all its delights—for him.

The little whimpering moans and cries she made when he brought her to climax.

All his senses came alive with the memories. Those memories were erased from him for a few weeks, but they'd come back in full force, stronger than ever, and he couldn't push them away any longer.

Stamping his feet on the floor with irritation, he marched to the bed and lay down next to her. She looked fast asleep. He shouldn't wake her and resisted with every ounce of willpower. Being in close vicinity to her must have calmed him some as, the next thing he knew, she stared at him with such hunger hours later and what followed was perfect in every way.

What was he to do? He couldn't push her away. They'd made love. He would be the worst kind of man to tell her to leave his home. Yet, could he stay married to her? Could he trust her?

He dressed while she slept on. Unusual for Gelsey to sleep late. She was always up with the birds. The ordeal must have taken something out of her. He didn't want to wake her to say good-bye and also couldn't look into her eyes yet. He needed time to think of what he'd done because he'd just made it harder to say good-bye.

Chapter Nineteen

"So, it's R2,000 a month and it has an open-plan lounge and kitchenette plus a bedroom and bathroom?" Gelsey had to repeat what the woman at the estate agent said in detail because it seemed too good to be true. Her salary was a tiny R3,500, so she would be eating baked beans on toast most days, but at least she wouldn't be living off of Evan when he resented everything she used and did in his home. She could start a new life for herself, learn to become strong and independent. Then he couldn't tell her to leave when she wasn't ready. Better to leave on her own terms.

"You can move in today."

Whoa! So soon? "And payment? It's partway through the month."

"Pro rata."

She'd have to ask Marissa what pro rata meant.

"Okay." She tried to sound sure of herself.

"You'll need a deposit of the full amount upfront and to sign a lease."

"Can I call you back in a minute?" The agent said it was fine and she hung up.

Marissa looked at her, an eyebrow raised.

"What?"

"Are you moving out for sure? Did it go that badly last night?"

Not bad at all. Heated tingles ran up her neck. Sensations from their early morning lovemaking slid through her body. "Um...I need to become independent. I can't hang onto him, be a leach—"

"Did he tell you to leave?"

"Not exactly."

Marissa gave her a look of disapproval.

"I can't force myself upon him. Please, help me here. What is a deposit, and what is pro rata?"

Marissa explained all the arrangements of renting her own place in detail. Gelsey nodded and bit her lip. She'd lived for six months in the human world, earning a junior salary and hadn't had any time to save anything. R2,000 wasn't much to lay out, but it was a huge amount for her. What could she do?

"I'll lend you the deposit. Not that I'm happy you're moving out, but I can't tell you how to run your life."

"I can't borrow money from my boss."

"Of course you can. I would pay you more if I made more. You're worth a million. I'm so much more relaxed when you're here. The last few weeks without you were hell, and I interviewed so many chancers. Could not find a single soul to take your place. Although I'd forgotten about you, you'd set my standards higher."

Gelsey giggled. "Thank you. I enjoy my job."

"So, phone her back and get your new place. I'll even let you leave early to move your belongings over."

"It's going to take much longer than my last move. Evan spoiled me with so many nice clothes, jewelry, and pretty girly things the first six months of our marriage. I have lots more stuff than before."

Marissa rolled her eyes. "You're crazy to leave him."

"I have no guarantees." Gelsey set to work on an arrangement. For once, they were preparing for a wedding. She took care placing the white Casablanca lilies in a pristine crystal vase alternated with some greenery. She breathed in the heady aroma of the perfumed flowers. There was no point in talking about it any longer. She'd made up her mind. The thought of sleeping alone churned her stomach and was one of the reasons she didn't cope well as a fairy returning from the human world. She didn't have the wild cats either and would miss out on spring. No, she shouldn't look back. Remaining positive was essential to her survival.

Wild Cats! She gasped. In all the stress of trying to reach Evan and make their love work, she'd forgotten about her promise to the queen to help the wild cats. Good thing she hadn't paid her deposit on the apartment. *Oh, dear!* She'd have to find a way to get there. She'd phone the conservation center in Kruger National Park to see if they had a job for her. It would be so much better to be far away from Evan so she wouldn't be reminded of how she'd failed and hurt him.

The only problem—how to tell Marissa she intended to move to Mpumalanga?

⋄

Evan held a letter, surprised at his steadiness as he read the crazy news.

In one day, Gelsey had upped and left, not to a flat somewhere, but was on her way to Kruger National Park in Mpumalanga Province.

He'd watched her pack her belongings into boxes and suitcases the night before but hadn't said anything. Instead, he'd slept on the couch, unable to be near her. She gave up too fast. What could he say? He'd said he wasn't ready for them, so he couldn't exactly plead with her to stay if he wasn't too sure himself if they loved each other.

It seemed they didn't if she could leave without a fight.

I've found a position at the Bushpark Conservation Center in the Kruger National Park in Mpumalanga Province. It doesn't pay much, but they were so thrilled to find someone who is passionate about the African Wild Cat. I'd forgotten about my promise to the queen to help the wild cats as a human. With this offer, I don't have to let her down. This may be my reason for coming back to the human world.

Marissa's not happy, but we'll keep in contact.

I want to say I'm grateful for everything you did for me, Evan. You changed my opinion of humanity. The way you treated me as your wife made me see the value of human beings. Before I was a little xenophobic. I despised humans. Now, I'm one of them.

All the best with your business. I will phone sometime to see how it's going.

Gelsey

That's it? It all came down to duty again. Duty to her queen. The one who had hurt her deeply.

If she wanted to follow the queen and her duty, he couldn't stop her. The magic alone had held them together. The sexual attraction wasn't strong enough.

He sighed and ran his fingers through his hair. Once again, his home seemed to echo emptiness with every movement he made. The choking sensation grasped him around his chest. He coughed and went to bed to try to sleep. He had to take it easy and not let the stress get to him.

Organizing a divorce was going to be stressful. He blocked out the sunlight streaming in from his window with his arm over his eyes—the winter sun always seemed to come in at a lower angle and beat down upon his bed. Most days, he would aim for the patch like a cat, but today, the cheeriness of it seemed to mock him.

"She's in hospital," his mom said, her voice shaky, her eyes big. "We have to go there right now."

"What's wrong?" he asked, his heart racing like crazy.

"There was an accident during hockey practice. One of the other kids swung the stick at her. They hit the artery in her neck, and...her face is in a bad way." She grabbed stuff as she talked then stood as if unsure what to do. "Where are the car keys?"

"They're on the hook, Mommy, where you always put them."

"Let's go."

The ride to the hospital was silent. What if Trisha died? They'd fought this morning. They always fought in the mornings because Trisha took so long to get ready for school and made Evan late and get into trouble. Everyone lumped them together because they were twins. When she got into trouble, he was part of it and vice versa. When she felt pain, he shared the pain. When he felt scared, she was, too. What would he do if...?

No, it wouldn't happen. Trisha was strong. She was a fighter. He'd toughened her up, wrestled her to the ground almost every day. He'd taught her how to punch like a boy—the reason she was so good at sports. His sister was the tomboy of the school.

Evan lay still on his bed. All he could hear was the swish of his blood pumping in his ears, slow and steady. Strong, not like Trisha. He'd failed her.

When they'd gotten to the hospital, she was already gone. She'd bled to death and suffered severe brain damage. From a hockey stick. To this day, he couldn't understand how his strong, crazy, happy sister didn't survive such a stupid injury. A part of him died that day, making him no longer able to love and believe in miracles.

And he'd thought Gelsey had opened that part of him again.

At the moment, he wasn't so sure.

Gelsey. With his help, she'd managed to obtain her driver's license the fourth month of their marriage. He'd spent many hours after work teaching her to drive. He was astounded at his patience with her.

She still didn't own a car. Her financial situation was bleak. He'd helped her with her bank account, so he should know. How was she even getting to Mpumalanga?

He sat up. Would she be safe? What means of transport was she using?

He slumped down again. Gelsey didn't want his help. She wanted to step out on her own. She didn't see any future in their relationship. He couldn't chase after her especially if he wasn't sure their love was real.

He just had to deal with this choking emptiness. Maybe after a few weeks, he would get over it. Never again, though. He wouldn't risk his heart with women again. He used to manage fine on his own. The casual dating he could do without, too.

One day, maybe, he would consider dating again—in the far distance when he didn't see Gelsey in every bird, flower, or sunrise or hear her in every soothing tune.

Ω

She should be petrified. She sat all alone on a Greyhound passenger bus with two empty seats next to her on the way to White River in Mpumalanga Province, not as a fairy but as a human. She would arrive at White River and then be fetched by her new boss for another long trip into the nature reserve. Thankfully, he'd footed the bill for her whole trip.

How she wished she could fly there in two days, stopping to rest at night inside a tree stump somewhere, instead of bounce around on a bus, looking down at the crazy drivers below. Many South Africans had very little care for road safety. She didn't know what the rest of the world was like, but she was certain of one thing—many of them had no regard for their own lives or the lives of other drivers. Especially, the mini-bus taxi drivers. They would drive fast along the highways with their vehicles crowded with passengers and overtake on a blind rise or curve. Her heart went crazy sometimes when the bus almost rammed into several of them. As for some truck drivers.... This side of humanity she struggled to understand. Fairies considered the sanctity of life of the utmost importance. Humans often considered making a quick buck more important.

Weren't the two very closely interconnected for humans?

So, why was she going to work at a conservation center for absolute pittance—a mere R1,500 a month? Okay, she would be given free board and lodging, so in a way, she would be better off. Good thing she hadn't signed her new lease.

Marissa had been tearful but hadn't pleaded with her or said anything nasty in retaliation. She promised to be back in about six months once she'd got a wildlife program in place for the wild cats. Marissa nodded but said she might have to hire someone in the meantime, as she wouldn't cope alone.

Oh, how awful she felt. Her boss had been the one to help her so much in her first few months in the human world. She would write her a long letter expressing all her feelings toward her and slot in a special gift. What that would be, she didn't know. She would be living away from decent shops, so she would have to make something.

The thought of saying good-bye to Evan had been too much to face, so she'd written him a note. She missed him already—missed their tender lovemaking, chatting with him, and even bumping into him in their home while doing mundane things. His company had been food for her soul in their first six months of marriage. She'd often followed him into a room and just hung around because she enjoyed being with him. He'd done the same.

She couldn't believe it was all over.

She had to start fresh and hope someday, maybe, she would find someone else to love. But she was wary. Human love was fickle. The hurt of breaking away was not worth the joy of those few short moments together. The memories would taunt her forever.

She swiped a stray tear away and blinked to focus on the road. Land streaked by, and she noted cows and goats along the way, wishing to break free of her bounds and soar into the sky or swoop down and pat a cow as she went past.

Why hadn't she seen any fairies along the way? That bit

baffled her. If she had touched the silver dust, she should be able to see all realms. She felt fully human and wondered if her ability to calm people with her gentle humming even existed anymore.

Had the silver dust not made her see everything? Did she really know what the silver dust achieved? She'd just assumed it would allow her to see things because of what Birdy had told her about her uncle.

Was she mistaken? Had Birdy offered her own opinion and not fact?

A tingle ran through her. Maybe her love for Evan had transcended all realms in its force. Maybe it wasn't the silver dust.

Why hadn't she realized sooner?

Here she was, traveling farther and farther away from him with every minute. A mixture of fear and excitement threaded through her. Could she have been mistaken? Maybe they could make the marriage work.

She stood up—as if the motion could stop the bus and turn it around. Another passenger seated behind her stared at her.

But Evan didn't even want her back. Yes, he'd wanted her body, but he didn't trust her. She had seen it in his eyes, heard it in his voice.

She sat down with a bump and flopped her head into her hands. What was she thinking? Their relationship was over. It had never begun to start with.

Chapter Twenty

The new job was thankless. After a week, Gelsey thought she might burst. She sat at a desk in an office with one tiny window at the top of the wall, which she kept open even though the winter air blowing in bit through her layers of clothing. She had been given stacks of files to go through to write a report on what had been done with the wild cats so far.

She'd asked to go find the cats but was told she wasn't a field worker. *Not a field worker?* Didn't they know her?

So, she sat, stuck in an office without much light or air, looking through hundreds of messy papers without anything solid on them. She'd found a few reports from field work and payments made for medical supplies and equipment to help the wild cats but it seemed very little had been done. Reading the papers and putting them into separate piles had taken the whole week as she'd had to throw so much away. At last organized, she was ready to write her report. She typed it up slowly as she didn't know the keyboard keys well yet and felt relieved fairies learned to read and write in their young years, else she would have been helpless. Her few months watching Marissa and doing basic clerical work had helped prepare her for this. Yet, was it all worth it?

After printing the report, she took it to her new boss in his office.

"I see." He stared at the paper for a long time, his gray hair contrasting his deeply tanned, lined skin. How come he got to go out to the animals and not she? His complexion and the fact he was almost never in gave away the fact.

"That's all I can find. I don't think much has been done so far."

He sighed. Was she going to lose her new job before she'd even started? Then she couldn't say she'd kept her promise to the queen.

He stared at the paper for so long, she shuffled from one foot to the other. His office had as much air and light as hers. If she didn't get outside soon, she would suffocate.

Why on earth did she feel she had to keep her promise to the queen? She cared about the African Wild Cat, but did the queen care about her? She'd sacrificed herself as a fairy, but she was no longer a fairy.

Tears pricked her eyes. This was awful. Everything around her seemed dark and pointless. Nothing mattered anymore. How could she go on like this?

"What do you propose we do for these cats?" He spoke, his expression open and friendlier than it had been the whole time since she'd arrived.

"I can't propose anything until I see where you have any cats under protection."

"We don't have any under protection. We don't know where they are."

She knew where they were. She could go to them straight away. She'd looked through the conference room window just a few weeks ago as a fairy. She could orientate herself to the spot where she'd cared for the two mother cats and tended to the wounded male cat.

He sighed again, raking his fingers through his hair. "Times have been tight. No one wants to volunteer to work with us since they can't survive on the salary we offer. You're the first person who's been willing to stay. I'm sorry I made you sit in that awful office for the first week, but I needed to see how determined you are about this job. Working in conservation isn't always glamorous. People think you're out there all the time with the animals, saving their lives, but there's a lot of paperwork and liaising with people. You have to organize fundraising events."

Gelsey nodded, weariness seeping into every pore of her skin. She much, much preferred working in the florist shop where she got to touch and smell the flowers every day, where she at least had Marissa to talk to, although her ex-boss was rather task-orientated and not the chatty type.

"But I can see you have the tenacity to stick it out. You've done very well in compiling this report. I appreciate your honesty in saying very little has been done as that's true. I need someone who is a realist. So, I want you to come up with a plan. We have a company vehicle for you. You may use it for personal use, too, a Land Rover Discovery. It's secondhand but in good condition. You'll be able to locate some wild cats and start monitoring them. The greatest threat to them is they are breeding with domestic cats. I don't know how to stop them from doing so, but you said you know the species well. With your expertise, I'm hoping you can come up with a solution that doesn't cost too much money. So...." He fumbled in his drawer and took out some keys. "Here are the keys for your Land Rover. It's parked out in the back next to the telephone pole."

Pinch me, I'm dreaming. She laughed, thrilled at having her own wheels and being able to go out in the field. "Thank you so much! You won't regret hiring me, Mr. van Schalkwyk. I'm going to save the wild cat for you."

"Good. Now, be careful out there. There are other wild animals. Speak to Sinenhle. He will get a shotgun ready for you."

"I will."

He went back to his work. Gelsey had to stop herself from skipping out the door to her new vehicle. Forget the shotgun. She knew how to evade wild animals. She already had on her khakis and hiking boots in hopes that one day, she would get the chance to go out. Little did she know how soon it would be and how much responsibility she would be allowed just for doing a simple report.

Oh, gosh, and she'd almost given up.

As she stepped outside, she breathed in the fresh air and jumped up, fisting her free hand in the air. "Woohoo!"

One of the cleaners smiled as she walked past.

Within half an hour, she navigated dirt roads in an unfamiliar vehicle, her arms aching and sweat beading her brow. Phew, what a tough job, but she wasn't going to let it faze her at all. At last, she got to do what she'd come here for.

She pulled up near to the spot where she'd watched the mother wild cats and opened the door quietly so as not to scare them away. She crept into the bush to find them.

The mother cats were gone, and their den showed signs of being abandoned for days. Her heart sank. What had happened in just a few weeks? Had Ronald not taken over caring for them? Had the queen not appointed someone else to take her place? She spent the next few hours battling through long grass and thorny bush to find them. It had been so much easier as a fairy as she could flit from bush to bush without bothering about thorns and wild animals or being affected by the harsh African sun on her skin.

In exhaustion, she slumped against a rock on top of a cliff and stared out at the country before her. What had she gotten herself into? What was she going to do if she didn't find any wild cats? Maybe it would take days. She just needed persistence—the same persistence her boss was convinced she had.

She wasn't going to give up, but questions kept popping into her head. Walking through this vast African bush and sitting here alone didn't feel too nice. She preferred being in the cozy florist shop, surrounded by flowers and potpourri dried rose petals, pretty scents, and wedding cards. She liked having a home to go to every night with someone to talk to who liked her and for the most part understood her.

Here, there wasn't a soul besides the cleaning ladies, a

cranky old reception lady—who buried her nose in dusty, bottle-green Reader's Digest abridged books and drank diet cola like fresh water didn't exist—and her boss. Somehow, the sweet woman she'd seen through the window as a fairy had gone. She thought her boss might be the man who'd hugged her, but she couldn't be sure.

She had to stick it out. She didn't dare go back to Evan; couldn't even live in the same town as him. There had to be a clean break, a new start. Where was some fairy magic to get her through?

The sun began to set behind her, and all of a sudden, the sweat on her skin cooled. African winters inland went from hot to cold in minutes. Time to go back to the car. She would keep an eye out for the cats with the late hour. Maybe they would venture out more.

She took a fast but stealthy hike down the hill to the Land Rover, glad she hadn't lost her strong sense of direction from her fairy days. It would not be a good idea to get lost here for a night.

The drive back along the dirt road in dusky light took every ounce of concentration and courage, but she made it safe, exhausted.

Once in her little room, the first thing she did was run a bath and peel off all the dirty, sticky layers. She sank into the hot water, her skin stinging, but she relished the heat. The last few hours, she'd been icy and shivery.

No wild cats. She'd seen a few buck and some warthogs as dusk came, but the wild cats had gone from this area. Tomorrow, she would try a new area. The conservation nature reserve was huge. The search could take months. She closed her eyes, but the tightness in her throat refused to go away.

The queen had no idea how different it was to be a human, especially a female on her own. How could she have made her promise such a thing? How could she have put such a burden on Gelsey when she'd sacrificed so much of her peace and happiness to obey the love commission?

Rebellion seeped into her soul. Not an evil, hateful feeling, but a pushing against the bonds, a realization of the unfairness of the whole thing. With it, a tiny thought blossomed within her. Who held her to this promise? Yes, she wanted to be good and do the right thing, but when it harmed her, what was the point? She'd become a self-serving human intent on self-preservation. There wasn't a single drop of fairy left in her, else she would be willing to do anything for the earth and for a promise.

What about her promise to Evan?

She jerked up in the bath, the water lapping over the sides with her sudden movement.

She'd made a promise to love Evan forever, hadn't she? And what had she done but run away? She'd made that promise way before her promise to the queen, but the queen had forced her to break it. Well, not exactly forced her. No one had ever forced her to do anything. She'd chosen to walk away from Evan because of fear of her own pain instead of putting him first. True human love put the needs of the one you loved before your own. It was willing to take the risk of loving without guarantee of being loved back.

That's what human mothers did countless times for their children. The sacrifice was the beauty of humanity. Yes, humanity failed sometimes, just like the fairies sometimes failed to save a species from extinction, but they kept on trying.

She'd run away a second time because she was unwilling to work through their issues, to face up to Evan's doubts and even to take a chance at love. She'd believed so strongly in the silver dust instead of Evan and the love she held in her heart for him. Maybe she did love him. She couldn't stop thinking about him. Life had lost its luster without him.

She wasn't miserable in her new job because of the work. Yes, she'd liked the florist shop, but sometimes she'd hated being stuck in the tiny shop, making funeral arrangement after funeral arrangement. The air con there had driven her bonkers in summer. How many times had she longed to take flight outside the city bounds and soar into the air currents?

No, she was miserable because she missed Evan. Whether

she loved him or not, she didn't know. Who was she to know? She'd only been a human for a few months, but she couldn't bear to be away from him. She wondered how he fared. Did he miss her? Was he happy? She'd never know those things by running away. She couldn't give him her love and share life with him when she was too afraid to try.

After hurriedly washing herself, she jumped out of the bath, rubbed dry, and dressed in some warm clothes. She packed her belongings. Tomorrow, she would return home, if he would have her or not. If he didn't want her, she would work her way into his heart again. She might not have gold and silver fairy dust, but she had the magic of care and companionship. Maybe that was all she needed.

Chapter Twenty-One

"Oh, my goodness, you look horrid." Marissa gaped at Evan and placed the dried grass she held down on the counter. "What happened to you?"

"I haven't slept for a whole week."

"Gelsey?"

"I'm so worried about her. I know she wants to be independent, but I can't help wondering what she's doing, whether she's safe in the bush, whether she has a decent home, whether she has food to eat. And I miss her." He sighed, not wishing to disclose his personal feelings to Marissa, but he felt desperate. No one else really knew his wife. He'd introduced her to his parents once, but he had the feeling they thought he'd made a mistake marrying so fast. Yet, they liked Gelsey. "Have you heard anything?"

Marissa shook her head.

"She didn't even leave a number. Nothing. I've done an Internet search to find the Bushpark Conservation Center in the Kruger National Park, and they have a few numbers, but I wanted to check with you first before I phone."

"Gelsey felt you didn't want her. She couldn't stay. I think she wanted to make a clean break, so I let her go without finishing her month off at her job and that's why I haven't tried to contact her. I'm a little surprised she hasn't contacted me at all, but I didn't want to push her."

"I didn't say she had to leave. I just said I wasn't ready to go back to the way things were before. I couldn't be married to a complete stranger."

"How can you live with her and yet not be married to her if you are married?" Marissa asked.

"I don't know. I didn't want to kick her out, yet I was unable to commit to forever. I wish she'd understood I was ready to start off slowly. I would have found a place for her to stay here in Newcastle. I should have said something. Now, it's too late."

Marissa shrugged. "I don't know what to say."

"Do you think she loved me, then?"

Marissa nodded. "That's one thing I'm certain of. She was crazy about you, right from the start."

"Right from the start?"

"After your honeymoon, she floated in the clouds. I know lovesick when I see it. I was once." She looked down.

"Does she still love me?"

"Why wouldn't she? Yes, you've hurt her by not believing in her, but if she didn't love you, why would she have given up her life as a fairy for you when she had no guarantee it would work?"

"You could be right, but I still wonder if it was just the magic."

"So what? We all need a little magic in our lives sometimes. Maybe magic's just what you needed to get you into a relationship in the first place."

Evan walked away from the counter and fiddled with some ornaments on a shelf at the far corner of the shop. Marissa had shot an arrow right into his heart like cupid, and he couldn't look at her. He had to process what she'd just said. If there hadn't been magic with Gelsey, he wouldn't have gone for her. He'd always believed in fate and destiny. Gelsey had been his destiny. His heart had hardened against love because of losing Trisha, but magic had broken through the hard outer shell to the soft part within.

He must love her still. He thought of her all the time and felt miserable without her. Even though she'd hurt him and run away from making it work, the worry for her safety and well-being consumed him. If she couldn't be strong enough to make it work, he would be the strong one. He had to rescue her from the queen's hold, too. That fairy queen wanted too much from her.

"I think I need to go find her."

Marissa looked up from her arrangement and smiled. "Well, it's about jolly time."

"I'll see you. Thanks for everything."

The older lady shrugged. "What have I done?"

"More than you know. And thanks for being there for Gelsey. You're a good person."

Marissa hit him on the arm. "Get out of here before I stick a flower up your nose."

"Going, I'm going."

∛

The bus ride to Newcastle went faster than the one to White River where she'd stayed. Nervous tension had her on the edge of her seat most of the time. A DVD played on a small screen at the front, and she squinted to watch it to get her mind off her arrival in Newcastle, but nothing helped take the butterflies away.

Good thing Mr. van Schalkwyk had appreciated the plan she'd drawn up over two days, working every day and until midnight. She had a breeding plan in place for the African Wild Cat. He needed to find at least two females and males and make an enclosure for them where they couldn't get out and go to neighboring farms and homes to breed with domestic cats. He'd even understood her reason for leaving. Not at first. But when she'd told him she'd been running away from a man and couldn't bear to be apart from him any longer, he'd nodded in agreement.

His immediate change in heart toward her leaving had convinced her he was the one who'd hugged the woman when she'd peered in the window as a fairy. Maybe he'd also run away from love.

Maybe magic still existed in her world. He'd let her leave with her full month's salary even though she hadn't worked a full two weeks. He'd also given her a lump sum to help her settle back in Newcastle, assuring her she'd done a wonderful job. Gelsey shook her head as she thought about it. She'd done nothing except create a simple plan—the very same plan she'd devised while in fairyland.

The bus dropped her off by a petrol station in town. How would she get to Evan's place from town late on a Saturday afternoon? Should she call him? As much as she didn't want to play the helpless female, she also didn't want to be so stubborn she couldn't admit she needed him a little.

She dialed his number on her cell phone. It rang and rang. Just as she was about to end the call, he answered.

"Hi." His voice echoed. He must be on speaker phone.

"Evan, it's Gelsey."

"I can hear that. Are you okay?"

"I'm fine. I need a lift home."

"Home?"

"I'm at the Shell garage in town."

"Which town?"

What was wrong with him? "Newcastle."

"What?"

"I want to come home."

"You'll have to phone Marissa. It will take me hours to get there."

Gelsey's heart sank. She didn't fancy waiting at a garage for hours as it got dark. Town central on a Saturday night wasn't the safest place for a lady. She'd have to phone her ex-boss. Awkward since she still hadn't sent her a letter of thanks.

"I was driving to fetch my woman."

She heard Evan but didn't know what he meant. *What woman?* "Who is that?"

Her heart sank even further, giving her a sensation of falling down a deep ravine. *Sandy. He's gone to get Sandy.*

"But I'll have to find an off-ramp somewhere to get off this highway so I can turn back to Newcastle. I'm two hours away from White River. I think I'll drive to Nelspruit, refuel, and make a turn."

White River. Nelspruit. Those names sounded familiar. She'd come from there hours ago. Was Sandy there?

"You don't have to come back for me." Her voice sounded small. Everything seemed far away.

"Now, I'm worried about you. Don't you get what I'm saying? I was on my way to check up on you and bring you home if I could. Well, seems like I don't need to do that anymore. Are you okay?"

Everything came back into focus—the bus offloading its passengers, the cars filling up with fuel, the shops around the area closing their doors to business.

"Oh, Evan. Of course I'm okay. For a moment, I thought you were going to Sandy."

"Sandy, the horse lady?" He laughed. "I dare not. You might pinch her or pull her hair."

Gelsey laughed, all the tension releasing. "I might just do that if any other woman comes near you."

"Don't worry. There's only one woman I want. I love you, Gelsey. I believe I always have."

She sucked in a breath. Everything turned crystal clear. "Me, too."

Epilogue

The marquee billowed in the wind that had picked up. A storm brewed in the distance. Not unusual for summer in Newcastle. Gelsey wasn't the least bit concerned. Even if it rained on her wedding day, she couldn't be happier.

She was marrying Evan for the second time. Yes, they were married on paper already, but this time, they would have the whole caboodle—the flowers designed by Marissa of course, the ceremony, the white beaded dress, a cake, and bridesmaids. The whole lot.

Evan's family had pitched in big time. They'd brought his little second cousins to be her bridesmaids and a flower girl, had paid for the caterers, and had organized a live band for the reception. Marissa had found the perfect dress for her and arranged the whole ceremony plus opened up her beautiful front yard for the marquee.

She ran inside Marissa's house to change into the wedding dress. She would say her vows to Evan in forty minutes. Vow to love him the rest of her life.

A few months ago, she'd doubted that was possible. Today, she believed everything was possible.

As she stood in front of the mirror in Marissa's spare room while the noise of people fussing about downstairs filtered in through the cracks under the door, she thought of the journey she and Evan had taken the last few months after they'd decided to give their relationship another try.

Some days had been hard. The first few days since returning from the Kruger, they hadn't been able to keep their hands off each other. The passion and sexual longing had seemed unquenchable. Then they'd struggled through some doubts, some teething pains. Living together with full knowledge of each other's faults had proved hard but also liberating. She had no more secrets. Evan knew everything about her, and she had discovered things about him that opened a heart of love for him she didn't think possible.

What a struggle to put her dress on. She should have asked for Marissa's help but didn't want to pull her away from the huge task of setting up the elaborate arrangements along the center arch of the ceremony area set up next to the marquee.

A tentative knock sounded on the door.

She held her dress over her as she couldn't clip it up at the back and said, "Come in."

Evan's mother, Sharon, entered. "How are you doing?"

"I'm struggling to hook the buttons at the back. The straps are twisted."

"Let me help."

"Thank you."

Sharon crossed the room and took over. Soon, Gelsey looked perfect. The older lady hugged her. "I'm so glad you decided to have a proper ceremony after all."

"Me, too. It's hard work, but it's worth it."

"I had to come and thank you."

"For what?"

"For giving me my son back."

Gelsey frowned. "I thought I was taking him away." She giggled like a silly fairy.

"You've put the light back in his eyes and the pep back in his step. The love between you is magic and has healed my son's broken heart."

"Are you talking about his sister's death?" Evan had sat her down a few hours after he'd come home from his trip to find her and explained why he'd been so frightened of committing to her in case she left him like Trisha had. It had all become clearer from then—the reason he'd felt so betrayed when she disappeared. Why he had struggled to trust again.

Sharon nodded. "On top of dealing with the grief of losing my daughter, I also lost a portion of my son that day. He closed himself off to everyone, even his dad. We tried everything, but he was totally broken. Trisha and he were inseparable. I don't know why she had to die, but I'm so glad he found you. I honestly didn't think he would have a normal relationship with a woman, but here you are."

Her cheeks throbbed with heat. "Evan changed my life forever, too. He taught me what true love is."

Sharon gave her hand a quick squeeze. "I'm so glad. Now, I'd better leave you to finish your preening. My son is sitting on the chair at the front of the little ceremony area, waiting for his bride. It better not rain."

Gelsey smiled and went to the window after Sharon left. She peered at the gathering clouds on the horizon. Summer rains— one of her favorites. The guests wouldn't like it but too bad.

There was another knock on the door. "Come in."

Evan stood there, his face puckered with worry. "It's going to rain."

She shrugged. "I don't mind."

"Your hair is so lovely curled and your beautiful dress. What about the flowers Marissa has spent hours setting up?"

"I love summer rain."

He came to her and placed his hands on her bare shoulders. She shivered with the pure delight of him sneaking a moment with her when everyone ran around downstairs preparing for their ceremony.

"I tend to forget sometimes you come from another world."

She snuggled her head upon the crook of his neck. They'd been so busy, having to prepare for their wedding, they hadn't made love in over a week.

He kissed her on the head. "I'm not supposed to see the bride in her wedding dress until she walks down the aisle."

"You could take it off."

He obediently unbuttoned the tiny clasps at the back Sharon had painstakingly done up just minutes before. What would his mother say if she knew? Feeling naughty and loving it, she rubbed her bare back against him. He ran his fingers all the way down her spine, making her shiver. Then his hands reached her buttocks, and he gave them a tight squeeze.

"We're supposed to wait until our wedding night," she whispered, her voice husky.

"Oh, but I can't wait," he teased, licking her earlobe. She turned her head round to stick her tongue in his mouth while she wriggled off her panties.

"Me neither."

She moved around again so her back was to him.

He reached forward and clasped her breasts from behind with both hands. She squirmed with the immediate sensation of arousal.

His trousers must have been dropped without her knowing because his hard cock pushed in between her buttock cheeks. He thrust up and down, glorious friction sending her to the roof. She squeezed tight and let out a sigh.

Flipping her around, he slid into her with ease as the moisture had already gathered between her lips. He pushed her gently so she landed on the bed in the room, hovering above her, lust in his eyes. She took in the vision of her favorite human, eyes wild with passion, face scrubbed clean for the ceremony. Her tongue came out, ready to lick him, taste him, and experience him to the fullest. Her wedding dress pooled at her feet, and he slid in and out of her with excruciating dexterity. She bucked toward his thrusts, squeezing her eyes shut as the pleasure reached sky-high intensity. To bring her to the utmost peak, he plunged his warm, smooth tongue into her mouth and pressed his muscular upper torso against her chest. His closeness, strength, and love infused her. Their intimacy and the sweet sensations rippling through her core brought her to wave after wave of climax. Panting, she opened her eyes. He smiled in his own lazy way, obviously satisfied, too.

"We'd better get ready to make our vows."

"I'm ready."

He flicked her nose playfully. "Not in the emotional sense, my faye. I mean, we'd better clean up a little."

Gelsey laughed. She soared on the wind currents and life was good.

~ABOUT THE AUTHOR~

Vicki is a total romance addict in almost every form. She's had several romances published in other genres. She lives in South Africa and keeps herself busy while working from home, writing blogs, and romance novels.

You can visit Vicki at:
www.vballante.blogspot.com

www.ingramcontent.com/pod-product-compliance
Lightning Source LLC
Chambersburg PA
CBHW060929120626
46557CB00003B/934